fostergirls

fostergirls

Liane Shaw

Second Story Press

Library and Archives Canada Cataloguing in Publication

Shaw, Liane, 1959-
Fostergirls / Liane Shaw.

ISBN 978-1-897187-90-6

I. Title.

PS8637.H3838F67 2011   jC813'.6   C2011-900075-X

Editor: Alison Kooistra
Design: Melissa Kaita
Cover photo © iStockphoto

Printed and bound in Canada

Second Story Press gratefully acknowledges the support of the Ontario Arts Council and the Canada Council for the Arts for our publishing program. We acknowledge the financial support of the Government of Canada through the Book Publishing Industry Development Program.

 ONTARIO ARTS COUNCIL
CONSEIL DES ARTS DE L'ONTARIO

 Canada Council   Conseil des Arts
for the Arts   du Canada

Published by
SECOND STORY PRESS
20 Maud Street, Suite 401
Toronto, ON M5V 2M5
www.secondstorypress.ca

To my mother who taught me to love language, my father who taught me to love learning, and to my many students who, although faced with the unimaginably difficult challenge of life without mothers or fathers to call their own, still managed to teach me lessons in strength, courage, and survival.

chapter 1

The school is staring at me. Rows of rectangle eyes blink at me in the sunlight, telling me to get my butt inside. I try glaring back, but I'm outnumbered. Another year of boring and stupid information shoved at me. Even worse, another year of boring and stupid kids who will:

a) ignore me,

b) get up in my face and force me to make them regret it, or

c) try to make nice with the new girl.

I vote for *a)*.

I landed here because pseudoparent number twelve decided I suck. Which works for me, because I decided that pseudoparent number twelve sucks also.

Nice when people agree.

School number thirteen. Not that I'm superstitious, but it fits.

Man, I'm sick of schools. They're all the same. Big boxes filled with lots of little slots where all the kids have to fit neatly. If you

1

don't just slide into place, you get squished and rolled around like a lump of Play-Doh until they figure out a way to squeeze you in. Or they just give up and send you off to another box with the same size slots that you still don't fit into.

I am definitely in the Play-Doh category, forced into the same slot in every single school I've ever had to go to. I get the same brilliantly original label every time.

Fostergirl.

They don't necessarily say it to my face.

Sometimes they say it beside my face, talking to my social witch, sorry, social *worker*, instead of me. *She likely failed the math test because she's a fostergirl. They often have trouble with math, you know.* For the record, I'm pretty good at math. I have to do a lot of counting to keep track of where I've been and where I'm going.

Sometimes they whisper it to other teachers or even kids, gossiping snakes hissing about things they know nothing about. *She may not completely understand what she's done. She is one of those fostergirls, after all.* For the record, I always understand what I've done. I always do it on purpose.

Sometimes they just stare at me, eyes convicting me without a trial. *Here comes trouble. She's a fostergirl.* For the record, that part is true.

Technically, I'm not even a fostergirl any more. My social witch ran out of lovely homes to dump me into, so, as of last Friday, I morphed into a grouphomegirl.

I'm pretty sure it's not a promotion.

The group home doesn't have "parents." It has "workers," which at least tells it like it is. Parents don't get paid to look after you. At least, that's what I hear. They pay *to* look after you. A completely different thing. Workers do their job and then go home and have a life. They don't have to pretend to be your mom and dad and don't even have to pretend they like you. That works for me.

My survival plan is to keep a low profile. I'm not very noticeable, anyway. One of my teachers once called me a dark horse. Never was sure what she meant and never was sure I cared, but I figure it has something to do with my looks. Can't be my sunny personality she's talking about. I am kind of a dark-looking person. My hair is black. I don't dye it like the goths. It came this way. It also came curly, which I can't stand, so I cut it short enough that it behaves itself and stops looking so girly. My eyes are super dark brown, almost black. I used to wear lots of black eyeliner to make them even blacker, but I don't bother any more. I'm more invisible without it.

I don't know who I look like. I don't know who my parents are or were. I don't know what country my ancestors came from or whose blood I supposedly have. One of my foster moms told me I look like a Heinz 57. Sounded to me like she was calling me a ketchup bottle, which kind of pissed me off. She explained that it was something people call dogs with so many breeds in them that no one can tell what they are. So, I guess I was supposed to be happy that she was comparing me to something that craps on the lawn instead of something you pour on your hotdog. Pretty sure it wasn't a compliment either way.

All I know about myself is what I overheard one of my pseudomothers saying one time on the phone. That they, whoever *they* are, found me wandering around with my brother, going door to door begging for food. That the cops were called and took us in…big-time criminals at the ripe old age of like three or whatever we were.

We ended up with our first pseudofamily a couple of weeks

later. I guess I should say families, because we weren't together. I never saw him again. It's no big, because I don't remember him. I don't remember anything. I don't even remember begging door to door or why we were doing it. I don't remember the first few pseudofamilies who got stuck with me. My brain is full of holes and all of my memories keep leaking out. I don't care. It doesn't bother me. It did bother my grade six teacher who wanted us to write an autobiography. She was pretty ticked when I only handed in one paragraph. She probably decided that I could only write one paragraph because I'm a fostergirl. Poor little girl. Nothing to write about. Boo hoo.

I've been standing here so long that I don't see anyone else on the steps. Great. Late the first day. Not a good start. Would have been easier to disappear into the woodwork if I got here on time. I promised myself I was going to keep it clean and follow all the stupid rules in this school so that no one would notice me. Not to mention the fact that I have to follow the rules or I screw up my probation.

"Hi! You look kinda lost. Are you new? Can I help?" I turn my head at the sound of an annoying voice that sounds like a chipmunk on drugs. I can't believe it. Not even in the building yet and I'm faced with *c)*, trying to make nice with the new girl. Man, can this day get any worse? It's not even eight thirty yet!

I look at her with my best dark look, rolling my eyes and shaking my head. No real eye contact and no conversation. Usually works with the chirpy types.

"I'm Rhiannon," she says, as if she thinks I might care. "I've lived around here my whole life and I know this school like the back of my hand." She kind of flicks her hand in front of my face as if she expects me to look at the back of it. I resist the urge to look at my own hand. I'm pretty sure I don't know what it looks like. I still don't answer, willing her to go away and let me get inside and get in trouble by myself.

"I'll take you in and find your schedule for you. We're late, but that doesn't matter much on the first day. They expect us to be late. Well, not me, because I've been here before, but they're kind of used to me coming in a little after the bell. I don't mean to be disorganized, but I help my mom in the morning and it takes forever and I can't always get here so early. It was easier when we started later, you know, but since they changed the start time I've been having trouble. I just act super sweet and friendly with the guidance people and they don't get too uptight about it. Are you in grade ten? You look about the same age as me."

"Yeah." I'm so amazed at how many words come puking out of her mouth that I answer without thinking.

"Perfect! We might even have some of the same classes, so I can help you get settled in. I imagine it must be tough being new. I've never been new so I don't really know what it feels like. I can imagine it because I have a pretty good imagination, or so my mother always says, although she's not usually complimenting me when she says it, but is telling me to stop being such a daydreamer and to focus on what's in front of me. Which right now is the school. Which we have to get into because we are getting pretty late, even for me. Don't want you getting in trouble on your first day. Especially not because of my big mouth. Which, by the way, I know I have. My mother again. I do talk a lot, which drives some people crazy. You just have to tell me to shut up once in a while and I'll do it."

She stops for breath and I realize that somehow she's maneuvered me to the top of the stairs. She's standing, smiling at me, hand on the door, telling me I can tell her to shut up. Usually I have no problem telling people to shut up when they get in my face. This time, I decide to resist the temptation.

"OK, let's head down to guidance," she starts again. Apparently she's filled her lungs up enough to start spewing out a new set of words. "There are four guidance counselors here; Ms. Smith, Ms. Beckett, Ms. Jackson, and Mr. Derringer, like the gun, which is funny because he's the only guy. Ms. Smith is the nicest and Ms. Jackson knows the most but Ms. Beckett usually does attendance, which is too bad because she's the grumpiest one…"

She keeps on babbling away until we make it to the office. Her voice stops dead when we hit the doorway where this woman is standing looking totally PO'd.

"Rhiannon. Not a very good start to the new school year. You aren't a freshman any more, you know." Typical teacher voice and typical teacher words. Is that what they learn in teachers' school? How to talk down to kids and make them feel useless?

"I know, Ms. Beckett. I'll do better. I promise. I'm just helping a new student get oriented, and it took a little longer than we expected." Rhiannon smiles sweetly. Her voice has morphed into this calm, mature-sounding tone that seems to slow the teacher woman down.

"That's all right. No excuses tomorrow. And you are?"

"Sadie. Sadie Thompson."

"Oh yes. You're one of the group home girls."

Grouphomegirl.

Fostergirl.

It's all the same to me.

And so it begins again.

chapter 2

There are six kids living in this group home. Six girls. Messed-up babes from all over the place. I haven't really talked to any of them much yet. The one sharing my room seems to like taking sharp stuff and decorating herself with it. Personally, I prefer tatts. I guess they cost a little more, but they last longer and look better.

I've only met two workers so far. One of them looks pretty scared and shaky about the whole idea of hanging out with a bunch of fostergirls-turned-grouphomechicks who are basically a bunch of whacked-out mental cases—except for me, of course. She might be kind of fun to mess with. The other one looks pretty mean and tough, like she isn't scared of anyone at all. She might be even more fun to mess with.

Not that I'm actually going to make the effort to mess with either of them. It's not worth my time. After my next birthday, I can apply for legal emancipation. Sounds fancier than it is. It just means that I can get my own apartment and find a job and not have to deal with anyone but myself. It bites that I'll still have to go to school until I'm eighteen because some politician with nothing better to do than ruin kids' lives got it into his pin head that kids are better off in school than out working. But I can still try to get out of the fostergirl crap and into a "supervised" apartment when I'm sixteen. I'm counting the days—using those good fostergirl math skills.

Meanwhile, I have to survive in this group home place. I have to keep my nose out of everyone's business and play nice with the workers. I have to go to school and not get kicked out or I mess up my probation.

I can do that.

Just so long as everyone else leaves me alone.

Every night here they have these house meetings. We all have to sit around and talk about what's going on and what isn't and make important decisions like who gets to use the bathroom first in the morning. Actually, not everyone is forced to go to every single bore fest. There are two little kids who live here; they're like ten years old or something. Their names are Krista and Kendra, I think. I don't know. I haven't really paid much attention. Everyone just calls them the Ks. They hang out together all the time and they don't have to do all the same stuff as us, like come to all of these meetings. Which doesn't seem fair to me. Why do I get punished just for being my age?

"I'm in grade eleven so I should have longer on the computer because I have more homework!" My roommate is whining again. Her name is Charlene something, and she doesn't talk much. Except to whine about needing everything she doesn't already have.

"So, I'm in grade nine, which means I'm in my first year of

high school. I need it more because I'm trying to get adjusted to a whole new kind of school, not just a new grade!" That one's Buffy. Really. She doesn't seem to have another name, which is too bad for her. Maybe if I had a name like Buffy I'd be a pain in the butt too. Not that Sadie is any great shakes, but at least I'm not named after some cheerleader who sticks vampires in her free time.

"We have a schedule set up. Everyone has equal time. We only have the two computers, so you will have to figure out a way to make it work. Problem solve."

"You problem solve. You made the problem by being too cheap to get us each our own computer!" This mouth belongs to Alisha—big, tough, and darker than me. It seems like it would be a good idea to get on her good side. If she has one, that is.

"House rules, Alisha. We talk it out and work it out. Buying new computers isn't an option." Sandi, the tough-as-nails worker lady, folds her arms and leans back in her chair. Brenda, the soft-as-toilet-paper worker lady, leans forward and opens up her hands toward us as if she wants a group hug or something equally repulsive.

"I wish we could buy you each your own equipment, but we only have so much funding for each of you. I know it doesn't seem fair, but we can find a way to make it work." She smiles at us, all kind of mushy eyed. Alisha swears at her, long and loud.

"Alisha." The word is quiet and Sandi doesn't move a muscle when she says it, but it still makes big Alisha get up and go to her room, shaking her head and muttering all kinds of really interesting combinations of swear words that I decide to store away and pull out when I need them. Brenda sits back and pulls her arms in, looking a little teary eyed. I don't think she's going to last long in this place.

"So, ladies, anyone have a solution?" Sandi looks at each of us. She has this way of staring at you that kind of makes you feel like lasers might start shooting out of her eyes if you say the wrong thing. I should figure out how she does that. It would come in handy at school.

"I don't need it." The words pop out of my mouth without permission. Maybe I'm channelling that Rhiannon kid.

"What do you mean, you don't need it?" Charming Charlene says, sounding like a total snot rag.

I ignore her. I have a suspicion that I'm going to regret opening my mouth. Actually, I already do regret it. Makes me too visible, my mouth all open and moving and making sounds like that. Stupid Sadie!

"What do you mean, Sadie?" Sandi asks this time. She doesn't sound like a snot rag. She sounds like one of those army generals in bad movies who can force anyone to do whatever she wants them to without ever raising her voice. I resist the urge to stand up straight and salute her.

"I mean, I'm not into computers." Shut up, shut up, shut up!

"We aren't discussing recreational computer time. We are talking about schoolwork." Brenda seems to have decided to try talking again. She isn't quite so warm and fuzzy this time. Trying to copy Sandi. The pathetic major trying to be like the general, but never getting the stripes. I don't answer. Just shrug, and wish Sandi would use her laser eyes to blast me into another dimension.

"Sadie?" Sandi again. One-word sentences that make you pay attention. I hate that.

"I don't really use the computer much for school. I don't always have one, so I just do without. You can split my time between the others. I don't care." Shut up, Sadie.

"Not a viable solution. You are in a new school. You can't be sure what's expected. You need your time. Everyone needs their time." I shrug again, and this time it seems to be enough. They keep on talking, and I just shut them all out. It isn't my problem. I don't care about computers. Homework is not really a priority for me.

I don't really *do* school. I go to school and I sit there and sometimes I listen, on the rare occasions that someone says something remotely interesting, but I don't *do* school. I don't worry about getting good marks and making my teacher happy by getting my homework in on time and making it all pretty. I don't waste my time reading all of the stupid books they give us. I can't think of anything more boring than actually reading a book from cover to cover. Why would I want to do that? Spend hours and hours reading about some imaginary person's life? Real life is pointless enough. Math is pretty pointless, too, but sometimes I do it just to keep busy. Every once in a while I pay enough attention in math to pass a test or two. I actually made it through most of grade nine, even though I floated through three schools last year. Then again, maybe that's the reason I made it through. No one knew enough about me to flunk me, so it was easier just to let me pass. Except in English class. Couldn't pull off a pass, so I'm stuck reading boring stories with a bunch of grade nine babies for another year, which is going to totally suck.

This new school is going to be no different than all of the rest. For the first while, the teachers will try to figure me out and complain that there aren't any decent records on me because I've been to so many schools. A few of them will feel a little sorry for me and try to give me extra help and maybe give me a decent mark that I don't deserve because it's easier than making a decision about what to do with me. A couple of them might try to push me a little and tell me I'm not meeting my potential and fail me to make me work harder. Another one of those brilliant motivational teacher strategies that work so well.

By the time all this happens, I'll be out of the group home one way or another and I'll be somewhere else, starting at a new school. I'm used to the pattern, and it works for me. No teacher ever really gets to know me well enough to really figure out what I can do. Which is fine by me, because I can't do much and I'd be just as happy to keep that my secret.

chapter 3

"Hey, Sadie, wait up! I have to talk to you!"

The voice chases me down the street. I try to ignore it, but it's loud and insistent and catching up to me.

How does that kid keep finding me? I leave at a different time every day just to avoid her. For a millisecond I consider starting to run really fast, but then I remember that I never run unless I am being chased by people who wish to do me bodily harm. I'm pretty sure Rhiannon doesn't have a pipe wrench or a knife in her hand, so I just keep walking and let her catch up. Maybe, after school, I can find a store that sells road maps. Wonder if there's a map store in this town? I might need to figure out a few different routes to school.

"Phew! I'm almost totally on time today! I can't believe it's only the second week of school and I've been late three times already! I only had to do lunches today but then Marie puked on the table, which is totally gross and disgusting by the way, and I had to clean it up, which put me behind schedule, not that I actually have a schedule yet but I am planning to have one someday. Anyway, I finally get that all done and then I forget my science homework and have to run back to my room which makes me later but then I saw you and realized that I'm not as late as I thought so I felt better. So, how are you?" She's still puffing a little. I can't tell if that's from running to catch me or if she's out of breath from babbling.

How am I? Good question. I have no idea.

"Fine," I answer, which is what you say when you have no idea.

"Get your science done?" she puffs. We're in the same science class, which made Rhiannon do a weird little happy dance when she found out.

"Sure," I lie. Science? I have a slight memory of the teacher saying something about reading something. Maybe.

"Great! Morton's a stickler. Anyway, see you in class!"

She runs into the school. I walk a bit behind, scanning the steps. I like to be the last one in the building. I time it just right, so that I don't have to go through the doors with anyone, but I still get in early enough to not be noticed by the attendance cops.

My plan doesn't work so well today, though, because I get held up at the door. Literally.

"What are you trying to pull?" Buffy, who seems to have mistaken me for a vampire, has me by the front of the shirt and is pulling me back down the stairs I've just gone up. I shake her off without any trouble and head back up, but she grabs me again. I could take her any day of the week, but I don't want the attention, so I hold back from rearranging her face.

"Back off. What's your problem?"

"You. Sucking up. Making everyone else look bad. Giving up

your computer time. What kind of crap is that?" She lets go, but she's still standing between me and the stairs. Time's ticking away. I look her up and down. Her eyes would definitely look interesting on the other side of her head, but is it worth the hassle?

"I don't suck up. I just don't do computers."

"Whatever. You need to know the rules at the house, or you won't last long."

"I know the rule about getting crap for being late for school." I point to the empty stairs and the doors that are about a second from being locked.

"Fine, but this is not over."

"I'm shaking, Buffy-baby." I shove past her, just hard enough to let her know I won't take her crap, and run up the steps. Late enough that I have to hit the guidance office. Can't plead first-day blues, either.

"I have English first period today," I tell Ms. Beckett, who likely already knows that, because she's got one eye glued to a computer screen and the other one staring at me over her ugly glasses. Her face could use a little rearranging, too.

"That would be English *nine* B?" She asks, even though she knows the answer. I nod, without looking at her, and she hands me the slip. I shove it into my back pocket and stomp down to the classroom. It's too late to be invisible, so I just plow my way in and sit down.

"Ah, Ms. Thompson, I see you have chosen to join us today. We are all truly honored by your presence," Mr. Wilson calls out to me from the front of the classroom, making sure everyone notices me. Wilson is short, bald, and nerdy, with a big nose he likes to slide his eyes down when he looks at you. His eyes are small and mean looking, and I don't think his mouth has a smile reflex. He was probably bullied when he was a kid and decided to become a teacher so he could try his hand at being the bully for a change.

Everyone laughs at his stupid joke. People do that. Laugh at bullies so they won't turn on them. I don't. I'm quite happy when they turn on me because I turn right back on them. I think about telling this bully where to get off, but I figure that would get me suspended, so I keep my lips shut. I've been suspended so many times that I don't much care, but I need to keep it together this time. A suspension could mess everything up for me.

"Ms. Thompson!" I look up, startled out of my thoughts by Wilson's loud voice. I force back a wince as Wilson puts a hand on my shoulder, keeping my eyes blank and wiling myself not to deck the jerk. "Ah, you are awake. I was afraid you had come to school to nap. Will you turn to page thirty-five, please. It's your turn."

"My turn to what?"

"Your turn to read. This *is* English class...or have you forgotten?"

Is this some kind of joke? This is high school, not grade five. The only people who read out loud in high school are the nerd babies who like to hear themselves speak.

"I don't want to read."

"That is unfortunate. Had you arrived in class on time, you would have heard me explain that I am choosing to listen to everyone read orally today, rather than depending upon volunteers. You don't have a choice in the matter."

"Yeah, I do. I choose not to read." I try to keep my voice quiet. The other kids in class are staring at the new kid, leaning forward a bit in their seats, hoping for some drama. I don't want to be the star of their show, but Wilson's making it hard to stay invisible.

Wilson starts turning red, and is kind of breathing hard.

"You are to read the third paragraph on page thirty-five immediately, or you will be looking at a suspension, Ms. Thompson!" Wilson raises his voice. Ah, the old teach-the-new-kid-who's-boss routine. Not a lesson I'm interested in today. I take a deep breath and slowly take the closed book and drop it on the floor at his feet. The kids all suck in a breath, ready to dive into the drama pool.

"You know what? I'll take the suspension. Anything's better than being here." I get up and kick the book across the room. I look around at the class full of blue-faced little nerd babies, sitting there afraid to breathe, eyes popping out of their brainless heads. I guess no one's going to try to make nice with the new kid in this class!

"Ms. Thompson! Office!"

"My name is Sadie. Get it. Ms. Thompson is some lady I haven't seen in about five years."

I head out into the hall. I choose not to visit the office. Since they're going to send me home anyway, I figure I'll save them the paperwork. I've always thought that telling someone who totally hates school that she'll be sent home if she does something wrong is a pretty stupid idea anyway. What do they expect me to do… beg them to let me stay in their dump?

I stand for a moment, looking around, wondering which way to go next. I don't have the school floor plan engraved in my brain yet. My lame brain. I haven't even made it through the second week without screwing up totally.

It's the teacher's fault. Where does he get off asking someone my age to read?

I start walking, trying to look like I'm heading somewhere, just in case anyone should happen to look at me and care. I'm not sure how to get out of here. I have a hazy memory of Rhiannon saying something about the back door being unlocked and not usually supervised. I don't know why she told me that or what she was talking about at the time. I never actually know what she's talking about and I try not to listen any more than I have to, but I guess sometimes she says something worthwhile.

I head toward the back of the school, keeping it all relaxed and casual so that no one will notice me. I seem to have become invisible again, because I find the door without Wilson or anyone else catching me. I push on it, hoping that Rhiannon wasn't just blowing hot air. It opens and I slip outside. I'm thinking now that maybe picking up the pace might be a good idea so that I can distance myself from the school before the suspension police catch me.

I make my way around the side of the school out toward the dumpsters, stopping for breath when I'm safely out of sight. The smell just about knocks me over and my stomach heaves a little. Another familiar smell cancels it out as my nose fills with secondhand smoke.

"Hey." The voice comes out from behind the smoke. It belongs to a girl I've never seen before. She looks older than me, but I can't really tell for sure because she's covered in makeup and piercings and just kind of looks like a really bad 3-D painting.

"Hi." Under normal circumstances, I wouldn't have bothered answering, but she's standing with three large guys who look like they might actually beat the crap out of me if I piss them off. I won't bother asking them to introduce themselves. I won't remember them anyway.

"You lost?" one of the guys asks, making the other two laugh as if he said something funny.

"No," I answer, trying not to cough as four clouds of smoke

add to my fog. I quit smoking last year. Not sure why I would want to make this life longer, but I did it anyway, just to prove that I could. I stare at all of them long enough that they decide I'm not going to scare too easily.

"You want a smoke?" The girl offers her already soggy cigarette to me, complete with her very own personal germs. And we just met. How sweet.

"Nope. Quit."

"Cool. So, do you have a note?" she asks, making an impressive smoke ring that mesmerizes me for a moment, so I don't answer right away. I never could do that. I tear my gaze away from the cancer circle and focus on her face.

"A note?"

"Yeah, a note that says you have a doctor's appointment and have to leave and that you have permission to be off today. So that the computer chick doesn't call your mommy and tell you weren't in class."

"No. I'm not skipping. I left because the teacher was being totally mental. I think by now I'm suspended." I give myself a mental punch in the head. I let myself get mad, and now the school has the upper hand. They'll call the stupid group home and report me, and I'll be in crap. Stupid! Maybe I should run back to class and pretend I was throwing up in the bathroom or something.

"Very cool." One of the guys nods, showing how terribly impressed he is.

"You can hang here. It's better than school," the girl is saying, but I've already lost interest in all of them.

"Thanks. Some other time."

I walk away from the smoke and give in to the urge to cough

as soon as I'm out of range. Man, I used to suck back a pack a day and now I'm like a smoke virgin again. I move down the sidewalk fast enough to get somewhere but slow enough that I won't draw attention just in case I'm visible again. I can't even watch for group home workers 'cause I don't know what kind of cars they all drive. Unfair advantage, I would say. Stupid Sadie. This town is definitely too small to hide in. Maybe I should head west and just find somewhere else to live.

I'm hungry now that I'm away from the dumpster smell. I check my pockets and I can't believe that I actually still have the ten I shoved in there last time my social witch passed me some cash. I take the risk of running into the corner store, figuring Sandi, or whoever else might be out looking for me, wouldn't have time in her busy day to buy chocolate bars or chips—which is what I decide to buy for lunch, because thinking about junk food makes me crave it.

Standing at the door with my food in its little plastic bag, I look out at the street. What am I supposed to do now? I don't even know where to hang out in this town.

I guess I'll just start walking toward nowhere, trying to figure out where nonpeople are supposed to go.

chapter 4

I finally decide to take my little bag of calories and fat and head down to the river bank where I can sit behind a tree and hide while I eat and try to figure out what to do or where to go next. Problem is, I barely even know where this stupid town is, let alone how to get out of it and back into something that looks like a real city.

Cities are so much cooler than these nerdy little towns. My last pseudohome was in a huge city. The school there is bigger than this whole town. Easier to hide in. Lots to do at night there, too. Always something going on and someone to hang with if you wanted to. It totally sucks that just because the police there were always picking on us fostergirls, I end up in juvie court and then dumped in this pathetic excuse for a town in an even more pathetic excuse for a "home."

If I try to leave, my social witch and probation officer will form their own street gang and try to find me. If they find me, the next stop will be a locked facility. At least, that's the threat if I mess up again. That's what they told me in court. Break probation, and they'll throw away the key.

Is refusing to read and kicking a book messing up in their world? Is a suspension considered breaking probation? Would my PO be PO'd enough to decide I'm too much trouble for the precious little group home?

My head is starting to hurt with all the thinking. I hate thinking. All of the thoughts get messed around and twist each other up until I have no idea what's in my head. I just want to close my eyes and shut off my brain at the same time. It's the same thing that happens when they try to get me to read all of that garbage in school. It all twists itself around until I can't figure out what I'm even looking at. Stupid Sadie.

I close my eyes and try to shut off my brain. I guess it works, because I kind of drift off to sleep.

"Ohmygod! There you are. I can't believe I found you. I looked everywhere in town, except here of course, but then I looked here and there you were. Or here you are. Whatever, I'm so glad I looked here. I heard what happened. I feel so badly for you. Wilson is so totally mean. I had him last year in grade nine and he is such a pighead that when my mother saw that I was supposed to have him again this year for grade ten she told the school that I have to be switched to another section, which is why I don't have English this term. Can I have a chip?"

My eyes fly open and my ears start ringing. Rhiannon flops down beside me and looks hopefully at my almost empty chip bag. I haven't even started to wake up yet or figure out what she's babbling about, but I catch the last word and figure she's asking for food. I hand her the bag.

"Finish it."

"Thanks! I'm starving. School always has that effect on me. I eat like a pig. I don't know how the skinny girls who are always on diets do it. I would just pass out from hunger, I think. I mean, I'm not skinny but I'm not fat either so I guess I'm lucky. Mom says I have a fortunate metabolism but that I might have a problem after menopause but since I'm like fifty years away from that, I guess I can eat chips in the meantime. Are you OK?"

"What? Oh, yeah, I guess." I kind of drifted off again while she was talking and almost missed the question.

"Everyone says he was being mean to you and that you were so tough and cool. I talked to Ms. Jackson about it, you know, the smart one, and she said she couldn't really discuss another student with me but that you should come and see her tomorrow when you get to school. You should do it, too, because she's really supportive and helpful compared to most of them. She'll help you deal with Wilson."

"I doubt I'm going to school tomorrow."

"Why, are you sick? Too much candy? I got totally sick one time at Halloween when I ate my whole bag of candy in one night. I don't even know why I did it. I knew better but I did it anyway. Man, I threw up chocolate and candy kisses for hours. It was so gross. Mom told me it served me right but she still gave me ginger ale and orange Popsicles, which are the things that I always have when I don't feel well. You might be OK by tomorrow though, even if you feel like crap right now." She puts her hand on my forehead for some bizarre reason and I move back. I don't think she's trying to hurt me or anything. I just don't like being touched. Ever. By anyone.

"It's OK. I'm just checking to see if you have a temperature. My mom does it by kissing our foreheads, even at my age, but

I figured that was inappropriate! Anyway, I thought maybe it isn't the junk food but that maybe you have the flu or something because I heard that like twelve kids in our year missed the second day of school because they were all sick."

"I'm not sick. I'm suspended," I tell her, standing up and hoping she'll get the hint that I want her to go away.

"Oh, I didn't know that. Well, I don't know if that means you won't be at school because our school usually does in-school suspensions unless the suspension is from violent behavior and I don't think kicking a book counts. If you had kicked Wilson you might have to stay home. Would it be a bad thing if I told you I wish you had kicked Wilson?"

A laugh flies out of my mouth before I can control it.

"I kind of wish I'd kicked him too."

"Actually, I'm glad you didn't because then you would be staying home tomorrow and that would suck. Our school's not so bad when you get used to it. Anyway, are you going home? I'll walk with you. We live like three streets over from MacAvoy House so it's not even out of my way. That's why I run into you sometimes in the morning. Actually, we could walk to school together most days if I could get myself out of the house on time!"

I look at her standing there all smiley, acting like it's normal that I live in a place called MacAvoy House that doesn't have anything remotely resembling a family in it. She probably lives in a big green-and-white house with a picket fence and daisies in the garden, with a mother in the kitchen baking pies.

And now she wants to walk to school with me every day. My plan was to walk to school by myself. That's always my plan. Alisha and Buffy go to my school, but we would never be caught dead walking together. We avoid each other as much as possible outside the group home. It's bad enough we have to live together. We don't need to hang out together. Don't need to draw attention to the whole grouphomegirl deal. Doesn't do much for the rep. Then again, I'm pretty sure walking around with Rhiannon isn't going to help my reputation much either.

"So, are we going?" she asks, starting to walk up the bank toward the road. I hadn't really decided what I was going to do yet, but it looks like she kind of decided for me. I can't really think of anything else to do inside the convoluted mess in my head, so I just follow her like the good little Heinz-57 mutt that I am.

She babbles away at me the whole way home. I'm not really listening, because I'm trying to imagine what level of trouble I'm going to be in. The answer hits me as soon as we get to the top of "my" street. Cecilia's car is parked in the driveway. The group home staff must be pretty excited to have called my social witch. I wonder if my PO is there too. Haven't seen him for a while. It'll be like a family reunion. My first one.

Rhiannon kind of waves to me and drifts off down the sidewalk, still talking to herself, which is probably an improvement over talking to me, and I go inside to face the music. Which is kind of a dumb expression when you think of it, because I like music, so facing it should be a good thing. I shake my head to clear it. That Rhiannon must be warping what's left of my brain with all those words.

Cecilia's sitting on the couch in the so-called living room, talking to Sandi. Buffy walks by and smirks at me. I ignore her so that I won't have to hurt her in front of the two women who could seriously mess up my already messed-up life. Alisha walks by the doorway and actually gives me a kind of sympathetic look. I think.

"Hello, Sadie. Come on in and sit down." Cecilia pats the

couch beside her. I sit in the chair. Sandi and Cecilia looked at each other in that way that adults do when they think we don't know they're mocking us.

"I'll leave you ladies to it," Sandi says. "Sadie, we'll talk after supper." Supper? I try not to moan at the thought. I told Rhiannon that I'm not sick, but ten bucks buys enough junk food that I don't want to eat again anytime soon.

"So." Cecilia looks at me with that "tell me all about it" look that never works on me. She isn't too swift.

"So what?" I answer like a bratty six-year-old. Cecilia brings that out in me.

"So," she kind of sighs. Poor baby. "Tell me about what happened today in school."

"Teacher pissed me off. He's a jerk. I lost my temper."

"We've talked about this, Sadie. You can do better. You have to do better this time. I'm running out of placements."

"Yeah, I know. Next stop, lock up."

"It's not quite that simple. If you violate the terms of your probation, a judge would have to decide the consequences, not me. According to your principal, you're getting an in-school suspension this time, which doesn't need to be reported to the probation officer because technically you are still at school. But an out-of-school suspension would have been a different story, and, from what I hear, you were pretty close to the line. I don't want you stepping over it. You don't want to end up in the juvenile justice system, Sadie. The group home is a good placement for you, and I don't want the staff to decide that you aren't trying to make it work. Placements are few and far between for girls your age. There aren't many group homes in this region. I don't want you to have to move so far away that you have to start over with a new agency and new worker."

"I'm almost sixteen. I just need to hang in until I can get out."

"We've been over this, too. You should stay in care until at least eighteen. You can have extended care past that also. Sixteen is too young."

"Says you."

"Well, after today's performance, I won't be the only one saying it."

"Yeah, well, whatever. It won't happen again. I'll handle it."

"Like you did today?"

"I said, I'll handle it."

"We need to problem solve this so you know what you're going to do next time there's an issue."

Problem solve. Every friggin' adult in our lives wants us to problem solve. They create all of the problems, and then they want us to solve them. What exactly does that leave the social workers and the teachers and the group home workers doing? Sitting around watching us do their work for them? Maybe I should grow up and be a social worker so I don't have to do any work. I can sit around and tell other people to solve their own problems.

"Sadie?" Cecilia leans forward and puts her hand toward me as if to touch me. I push back against the chair, and she seems to get the message.

"There's this guidance lady at the school. A friend of mine told me I could talk to her." It's a flash of genius. Thanks to Rhiannon, who isn't exactly my friend.

"All right!" She sounds excited. I should feel guilty, but I don't. "A friend. Great! A guidance counselor. Even better! That sounds like a positive first step. You can speak with her tomorrow during your suspension. You'll be spending the day in guidance anyway, so you can fit in some talking as well." She stood up to go, seeming pleased that *we* have the problem solved. I stay sitting until she leaves and then go up to my room, hoping that Charming Charlene isn't there.

I catch a break for the first time today, and the room is empty. I sit down on "my" bed and close my eyes. I hate this place.

"Crappy day?" I open my eyes. Big Alisha's leaning against the doorframe, arms folded. I bet teachers don't mess much with her. She looks like she could drop kick Wilson from here to wherever the next pathetic little town is.

"Yeah. How'd you know?"

"Word gets around. Wilson's a prime number-one jerk. I have better names for him, but I can't say them because Buffy is sniffing around trying to get people in trouble. You have to watch out for her."

"Yeah, well, my day started out with her trying to throw me down the stairs at school."

"Hah, bet you knocked her on her butt instead." She laughs. I don't.

"What's her problem, anyway?"

"She's one of those depressed maniacs. I have other names for her too, but I'll tell you later."

"Depressed maniacs?"

"Yeah, you know, nuts. One minute she's all lovey-dovey and trying to look after everyone, and the next she's running around trying to kill you."

"I've never seen her acting lovey or dovey." Why am I still talking?

"She mostly does it with the Ks. Thinks she's their momma or something. She likes kids who are younger or weaker than her or whatever. Probably makes her feel big and special. She hates me 'cause I'm just so much better than her. Probably hates you now, too." She smiles like she's complimenting me.

"She says I don't know the rules. You know the rules?"

"Only rule I know is you look out for yourself and don't listen to anyone else."

"Sounds like a good rule."

"Yeah. Not sure what Buffy's rules are. I don't listen to her much. Too much of a headcase."

"I don't have time for headcases. My life is messed up enough."

"Mine too. I'm here, aren't I? Not exactly a place where they put you as a reward for good behavior." She laughs at herself again. This time I kind of laugh, too.

"You been here long?"

"Forever. Six months."

"Sounds like forever. I don't want to stay that long."

"You got family to go back to?"

"No, you?"

"Mother. She's drying out. For about the millionth time. They keep taking me away even though I'm old enough to handle her. I'm old enough to deal."

"Know what you mean. I'm trying to get early-out."

"You sixteen?"

"Almost."

"What'll you do?"

"Get a job. Apartment. You know."

"What about school?"

"They say I have to stay until I'm eighteen, but I can make them ask me to leave before then. Except I need to keep it clean until I'm out of care. Which means sucking it up in Wilson's class." I close my eyes at the thought. I'm not going to read out loud to him or anyone. I have to find a way around it that won't get me in any more trouble…at least for a few months. Once I'm out, I'll come back and kick some butt. Then they'll kick my butt out the door and I can get on with my life.

"Well, good luck with that. Gotta go. See ya around."

"Yeah." I kind of wave and flop down on my bed. This is not going to be fun.

I make it through the rest of the day without having to talk about Wilson too much more. I guess Cecilia showing up on the scene made Sandi figure she's redundant so she left me alone. Anyway, I stay in my room all night, so I don't run into anyone else who might have an opinion about my life. Charlene comes back but doesn't bother to talk to me. Guess she can't find anything to complain about. She also doesn't seem to care about my day, which is fine because I don't care about hers, either. Makes the room nice and quiet.

I have a bad feeling that life around here isn't going to be quiet very often.

chapter 5

By eight the next morning, my bad feeling is a reality. Rhiannon
has somehow managed to get herself out of her door in time to be
standing in front of the group home when I drag myself outside
to face the dreaded in-school suspension. I have never had an
in-school before. All of my other schools were pretty happy to
have me out of school, which worked out nicely for everyone. The
staffroom devils at this school have come up with a much more
evil form of torture. Now I have a suspension but I have to go to
school and be watched all day, so I'll have to do a really good job
of faking my work. Unfair on every level.

"Don't worry, Sadie. Lots of kids have in-school suspensions
at our school. I've never had one but that's because I'm a total suck.
I don't have the guts to do anything remotely considered bad. Not
that I think you're bad or anything. It's just that my mom has this
hyperactive sense of right and wrong that she totally passed on
to me and besides she would basically kill me if I got in trouble

at school. Not that she would ever actually hurt me or anything. It would just be metaphorical. Like we learned in English class."

"What?" All I hear is that someone is getting killed in English class.

"Oh, nothing. I'm just babbling as usual. Anyway, everything will be fine after today. No one will think bad things about you or anything. It won't stop you from making friends or fitting in or whatever."

"I don't make friends and I don't care about fitting in."

"Really? Oh, I kind of thought we were becoming friends." I look at her like she's grown two heads, which would have been a total disaster because then she could talk twice as much. I know that I let Cecilia think that Rhiannon and I were friends, but I didn't mean it. Friends are just another complication in an already complicated life.

Rhiannon looks kind of bummed out, and I feel almost sorry for her for a second. I don't know why she would want me to be her friend, anyway. I'm not exactly soft and comfy cotton-candy friend material. I'm made of something a little harder and rougher than that. More like peanut brittle. The kind that breaks your teeth.

"It's not that I don't want to be friends. I just don't have a lot of experience with the friend deal. Moved around a lot." I'm not sure why I'm saying this. It's just that she's got this wounded-puppy routine going on, and, being a member of the dog family myself, I feel like I should do something to make her feel better. Except that I suck at this kind of stuff. I do a shoulder shrug so she'll know it's not a big deal. Doesn't work. She does a little happy dance and even claps her hands, like I handed her money or something. All I gave her was a double negative.

"Oh, well, that's OK. I'm not exactly an expert in the whole friend department myself. I had a best friend last year in grade nine but she moved away. She also moves around a lot. I don't. I just stay right here while everyone around me moves around a lot. You want to know a secret? Well, it's not really a secret because everyone knows about it pretty much. Most of the time I feel like I don't really fit in either, which I know sounds weird because I've lived here so long, but I don't always act like the other kids my age. Actually, I almost never act like the other kids my age. It's not that I don't want to, but I can't seem to figure out how. I talk too much and think too much and have kind of weird interests and people think my house is full of weirdness and stuff so maybe we could sort of not fit in together." She looks at me with those puppy-dog eyes. Not the Heinz 57-lost-mutt variety, but the cute-little-furry-pooch-wanting-a-treat kind.

"Sure." I really have no idea what I'm agreeing to, but it seems to make her happy. It even makes her quiet for the last few minutes of our walk, which makes it worth it…so long as I haven't accidentally agreed to go to a pyjama party or something equally repulsive.

We make it inside the school without running into Buffy or anyone else who is trying to make my life more useless than it already is. A few people stare and point when we walk by, but I ignore them and Rhiannon doesn't even notice them, so it dies down pretty quick. We part ways at the guidance office where Ms. Jackson is standing waiting for me. I can't remember if she's the nice one or the smart one. It doesn't really matter, because at least she isn't the attendance queen who gets her jollies from making difficult lives more difficult.

"Hi Sadie. Come on in. I have a desk set up for you outside

my office where you can work for the day. Your teachers have dropped off your assignments. I'll be seeing students throughout the morning but I'll have some time at mid-morning break and lunch if you need help. I also have a free hour this afternoon if you want to talk to me about ways of getting more settled in."

"OK." So far, this is not what I expected. No lecture. No principal telling me that I should be a good little girl if I want to stay in the school I hate. Maybe that part comes later.

I sit down at the desk she put there for me and look at the stack of work. The teachers have even been kind enough to provide me with extra textbooks just in case I forgot mine. Which I did. On purpose. Man, this place is not like my last school.

Science. Read chapter two and answer questions one through twenty-four. Yeah, right. English. Read two chapters and sum... sum...well, do something to them that would be a total waste of my time. Nothing from gym class. Too bad. Wouldn't mind going for a walk to the store for exercise and chocolate. Math. Questions one to forty. All review stuff. Adding, subtracting, integers, and some algebra. I might do that. At least some of it, so no one can say I'm not working.

I spend the first part of the morning doing math equations as slowly as possible. Kids go in and out of the offices talking to the guidance people. I wonder what they all have to talk about. Do they all hate their English teachers too? Ms. Jackson pops her head out once in a while to check and see if I'm working. I don't look at her. Just keep my head down and my pencil moving.

I'm busy drawing a really excellent picture of Wilson, complete with horns and a lovely tail, when a voice jumps at me.

"Are you done all of your work?" Jackson snuck up on me and is looking over my shoulder. I hate when teachers do that!

"No, just taking a break." I still don't look up, but I stop drawing and start making it look like I'm finishing my math.

"Do you need help with anything?"

"Nope."

"Well, come on into the office for a few minutes."

"I'm OK."

"I'm not actually giving you an option."

Of course not. Now it would come. The TALK. We would discuss the rules of the school and the Code of Conduct. I might even get the chance to write it out ten or even fifty times so that I would really, really understand it. Peachy. I follow her into the office and she closes the door behind me. It has a big window in it so people can see us but not hear us, like we're in one of those old silent movies except that we're in color.

"So, Sadie. Kind of a rough start to your year."

"No big."

"Well, not too big, but big enough. Mr. Wilson is pretty upset. I know it must be tough for you, but we have to figure out a different way to deal with things." Here comes Chapter Two. How she read my records and knows I'm a poor little fostergirl and how tough my life must be and how I have to try extra hard to do my best so I can stay here and how I have to problem solve for the future. That she knows I had problems in my other schools and how this school isn't going to tolerate this kind of behavior. How she knows I'm still on probation and that I'd better watch my step. This might even be when I get to meet the principal up close and personal so she can add in her own threats. I try not to yawn. I have so been here and done this before. I fold my arms and lean back—might as well get comfortable until the lecture series is over. I have nothing to say and don't really need to listen.

"Can you read this to me, please?"

"What?" Now she has my attention.

"I said, could you read this to me, please."

She's holding out the same stupid book that Wilson asked me to read. Is she totally kidding? Is this her idea of a joke? Is she trying to get me kicked out?

"I don't like to read out loud." My arms stay folded. She keeps holding out the book.

"It's just you and me here. Mr. Wilson does have the right to ask you to read in class. I just want to understand what the problem is."

"There isn't a problem. I just don't read…out loud, I mean." She's really pissing me off. I want to swat the stupid book out of her stupid hand. What is it with this school? Do they have some sort of reading-out-loud fetish? I haven't had to read to anyone since I was like eight and I don't even remember doing it then. They always just leave me alone. This babe needs to back off!

"I just want you to try a few words. It's not a big deal. I just think you need to get comfortable with the idea."

"Not right now." Back off, back off, back off, back off! My eyes close and my head shakes back and forth. I hear the book close with a thump. I open my eyes to see her putting it on a desk.

"OK, Sadie. Another time. For now, I'll ask Mr. Wilson to give you some time to settle in before he asks you to read again. All right?"

I look at her and nod, totally confused. What's going on here? Did she just say she's going to tell the teacher to back off me? I thought teachers always ganged up together to make sure we don't get the upper hand. Why would Jackson tell Wilson to give me a break? What kind of setup am I walking into here?

I spend the rest of the day trying to figure out what the master plan is and pretending to finish my work. My suspension ends without me ever meeting the principal and without anyone reading me the riot act.

What kind of lame school is #13 anyway?

chapter 6

I wake up in the middle of the night, sweating like a pig and shaking like I'm afraid of myself. I sit for a minute in the dark, trying to remember where I am. It's so black in my room. The night-light burned out ages ago and no one replaced the bulb. I take my blanket and wrap it around me to keep myself safe from things that hide in the dark. I tiptoe out into the hall, staying really quiet so I don't wake my brother up as I sneak past his bed. The house is so quiet. I don't make any sound at all moving down to the door at the end of the hall. I open it carefully so I won't get in trouble. I sneak over to the side of the bed and reach up to touch her on the arm.

But she isn't there. No one is there. I run downstairs to see if she's in the kitchen. Maybe she'll make me a sandwich if I tell her how hungry I am. I go to the kitchen. She isn't there, either. Or in the living room. Or in the basement. She isn't anywhere. It's just us. And I'm hungry.

I open my eyes, my stomach grumbling loud enough to wake me. I shake my head at the stupidity of the dream. I have it all the time, a nightmare about a stupid little kid having a nightmare and running around looking for her mommy. I always wake up, all sweaty like the kid in the dream and hungry, too. I've never figured out if being hungry makes me have the dream or if the dream makes me hungry. It's a stupid dream, anyway.

I sometimes wonder if it isn't really a dream, but a memory. I don't really have any memories when I'm awake, so maybe I get them when I'm asleep. But every time I wonder that, I also wonder if I'm just making up a memory because I overheard the big sad story of how I'm this poor abandoned kid. When I'm awake and not hungry, I don't remember anything at all about being a kid. I can't tell you what my mom looked like or my dad. Or if I even have a mom and a dad. I mean, I know I had them because I didn't come out of a test tube or whatever, but I don't know how long I had them. I could ask Cecilia, and she would have to tell me, but I haven't asked her. I'm not sure I'm interested.

I don't know if I have any other family floating around. My brother disappeared into the system and any other relatives kind of disappeared off the face of the earth.

I don't care. I don't need them. I just wish the stupid dream would stop waking me up. I have enough trouble staying awake at school without dumb little kids coming to me in my sleep.

At least no one's in the room. I have it all to myself. It's been that way for almost five days, ever since Charlene decided to carve herself a bed in the loony ward at the hospital. She got kind of carried away with her skin designs and really managed to hurt herself. They took her in for one of those ten-day-psych-evaluation things to see if they can figure out what her problem is. As if they could figure a whole person out in ten days.

They sent me away for one of those once. I was like ten or eleven. They sent me there because I stopped talking. Not sure why this was such a problem. No one listens to me much anyway. The thing is, I didn't have anything to say. I was in a new pseudohome and I guess the new pseudoparents were the sensitive type and were offended when I didn't answer their eight million questions. They kept asking me if I was missing my other foster family. Which is a useless question, because it doesn't have a right answer. If I didn't miss them, that would mean I should be ready and willing to play nice with the new ones. If I did miss them, that would be pathetic because I couldn't go back. They didn't want me and that was fine by me. I mean, I had been there longer than most places…almost a whole year, I think…and it wasn't totally bad to have time to get used to a place and all. But it's not like I was part of the family or anything, like they were my parents and cared about me. I mean, when a real mother gets pregnant, she doesn't decide to get rid of her older children, does she?

Anyway, I just decided that, since I didn't have any say in my life, I wouldn't say anything. This decision got me dumped in an evaluation bed where I had to hang out for a week or so listening to strangers try to dissect my so-called life. They talked at me a lot and tried to get me to talk back. After a while they gave up. What they didn't know about me, even after all their dissections, is that I listened when they thought I couldn't hear. I heard what they said about me when they decided to ship me off to a different foster home where the "parents" were trained to deal with "problem" children like me.

My "problem," according to the so-called experts, is that I'm passive-aggressive and I have attachment disorder. I looked it up, and it basically means that I quietly tell people where to get off and I don't care whether they like me or not when I do it.

I wonder if Charlene is going to say anything that will enlighten everyone so they will be able to figure out why a seventeen-year-old who lives in a useless group home and who, according to Alisha, had the crap kicked out of her regularly by her parents when she was a little kid, would be totally screwed up. Not exactly rocket science. Maybe she'll get lucky and they'll fix her up and she'll live long enough to go after her parents for what they did to her.

One of the Ks is around the age I was when I did the hospital gig. I don't know if it's Krista or Kendra. They both seem really young for the group home scene. I don't know why they're here and haven't bothered to ask. They're pretty tight for fosterkids. Just keep to themselves and seem to keep out of trouble. Kind of sucks for them that they ended up here. But they stay out of my way, which is all I care about.

Now that the whole suspension deal is over, school has kind of settled down a bit. Jackson seems to have done what she said she was going to do. She's breaking all the teacher rules. It's almost like she actually wants to help me out or something. None of my teachers are getting too much in my face. Wilson backed way off and just bugs me when I forget my homework on the kitchen table. He doesn't ask me to read any more. He has enough geeky little grade nines who are willing to show off their pathetic reading skills that he doesn't need me anyway. I listen to them enough that I don't need to bother reading the book.

Math class is still OK. We're still doing lots of real math, like numbers and equations and things, so I'm keeping up pretty much.

Gym class is OK, too, because I just keep my mouth shut and follow the directions. I got in trouble a few times for not bringing my gym clothes or whatever—I don't do change rooms—but I just kept on telling the teacher that I was confused by the whole tumbling timetable deal and she eventually gave up bugging me, so now I don't have to drop the class. I wasn't actually totally lying about the timetable bit. Don't know why they can't just teach the same crap at the same time every day so we don't have to look like idiots when we show up in the wrong room half the time.

Science class is different. Rhiannon somehow managed to make sure we're desk partners. This means I don't really hear much of the lesson because I have a running commentary going on in my ear. It doesn't matter, though, because somehow Rhiannon manages to do her homework and she has no problem with me copying her answers. She says something like that's what friends are for.

I don't actually know what friends are for. I know everyone seems to want them, but from where I'm sitting they cause more problems than they solve. They seem to hang around a lot, getting in your space and interrupting your life. They make noise. They make you feel guilty when you copy their notes and don't give them anything back.

"I don't mind, Sadie. I'm pretty good at science for some strange reason because I'm not all that good at math. It might be on account of my ADHD. Well, no one knows for sure if I have it because mom isn't convinced because she says I can concentrate when I want to but some of my teachers decided I have it because I can't seem to stop talking in class. They say I have an attention deficit which is funny because my problem is really more of an attention surplus. I have too much and I can never decide what to focus on. I'm not terrible at math but not wonderful either but I love science. It's so interesting to try to figure out why things happen the way they do and to see how ideas change over time. I watch every science show I can find on TV and even joined the science club in elementary school but I didn't join it in high school because last year when we were in grade nine my friend Ginny told me it's for geeks and since I am already kind of a geek I didn't want to get any geekier, especially with Ginny gone and me without much in the friend department although now I have you so maybe I'm not so pathetic after all. Do you think I should join?"

"What?" I'm still back at ADHD. Sounds like a disease. Hope it's not catching. I have enough problems.

"Do you think I should join the science club?"

"Sure." I have no idea what the science club is.

"OK, I will. Thanks for the advice, Sadie." She turns back to her science book and carefully writes the answer to the next question, keeping her book where I can see it.

"So, do you want to come over after school?" she asks me at the end of class as we're packing up our books.

"Come over where?" She looks at me and laughs.

"To my house, of course. My mom won't mind. You might have to help me get the kids a bit organized but then we could hang out and finish our homework before supper."

"Supper?"

She laughs again, shaking her head.

"Yeah, supper. I'm inviting you over for supper." She says it all slow and careful as if she's talking to someone who doesn't speak English.

"I don't know. I guess I can do that." I know I sound brain dead but I actually don't know. I don't get too many invites and I don't know the rules. Do I have to ask permission? Or do I just tell the group home that I'm not coming home for supper? I try to remember if any of the other girls have missed a meal since I moved in.

"Of course you can do that. Just call the house from my place and let them know you're staying. My mom can even talk to them if you want."

"No, I think I can manage a phone call."

"Excellent. Let's go!"

So, I'm not exactly sure how I ended up here. Walking down the sidewalk, with someone who calls me her friend, to have supper with a bunch of someones I don't even know.

Maybe I've finally lost the rest of my mind.

chapter 7

There's no maybe about it. I have to be without a mind to have walked into this place. Just when my life gets a little bit quiet, here I am in the middle of the Third World War. I stand in the front hall of the house, which is not green-and-white at all, and try to disappear into the shadows before anyone notices me.

It's a total nuthouse. Rhiannon swoops in to what is probably supposed to be a living room but looks more like a daycare. Toys everywhere, and I mean everywhere. On the floor, on the couches, on the shelves, on the coffee table, under my feet, and one that is flying through the air toward my head. I duck and it bounces off the front door and onto my foot. I can't tell who the pitcher is. There seems to be a pile of little kids jumbled around the room making a mess. Well, that's what they were doing when we first walked in. Now they're all screaming and crowding around Rhiannon like a swarm of bees around a smelly flower. I think about coming to her rescue, but since I've always been basically afraid of anyone under the age of twelve, I decide to stay put.

"All right, all right everyone. I have to introduce you to someone." Rhiannon separates herself from about a dozen sticky little hands and looks at me. I kind of shake my head and reach back to grab the doorknob in the hopes of making a quick getaway. As my hand touches the handle, it turns on its own and the door opens suddenly, making me fall backwards.

"Oops, didn't know you were there. Sorry!" I'm stopped from hitting the floor by a man who drops several bags of groceries to catch me. He has me by the arms and I shake myself free, trying not to seem rude.

"It's OK." I'm still standing in the hall. Rhiannon has managed to pull herself completely free of small bodies by this point and is standing in front of me, laughing.

"Hi Daddy. This is my friend, Sadie. From school. The one I told you about. She's here for supper."

"Well, then I guess I'd better pick supper up off the floor and get into the kitchen. Where's your mom?" I wonder the same thing. I mean, all those little rugrats can't be here alone, can they?

"Right here. Watching the crew from the dining room. I'm on the phone." A woman who is obviously Rhiannon's mom comes into the room. She doesn't look anything like I'd imagined. In my head she's been kind of a big, comfy-looking lady with an apron on and gray hair in a bun, with pieces hanging down on a face that has flour on both cheeks from baking pies. This lady is nothing like that. She's small and kind of tidy looking, with jeans and a sweater on. She has dark, reddish hair, like Rhiannon's, and wears it in a ponytail. She doesn't look like she's ever baked a pie and seems more like someone who should be out riding her bike than refereeing a room full of terrifying toddlers.

"Hey Mom! This is Sadie. She's staying for supper." It's at this moment that I realize Rhiannon hasn't even told her mom she's inviting me over. I'm totally embarrassed and start making up excuses to leave, inside my head, so that I can get out of here before her mom kicks me out.

"That's lovely. I'm really happy to meet you. Come on in out of the hall. Rhiannon, why don't you two go up to your room, and I'll call you when I need you?"

"But shouldn't I be helping with the gang?"

"I think your dad and I can manage for tonight. You two talk or do your homework or whatever you need to do. I'll get your help a bit later." She smiles at us both, and it kind of makes me want to do whatever she tells me to. Which makes me mentally punch myself for being sappy. I don't even know the woman! She probably has a rolling pin hidden behind her back that she's going to use to persuade these legions of messy children to tidy up the living room.

Rhiannon and I head upstairs, trying not to kill ourselves walking through the mess of plastic cars, stuffed toys, and a few dolls that seem to have been decapitated. I wonder about her mom. I couldn't remember any of my pseudomoms tolerating anything close to this kind of pig-sty. Well, maybe that's a little harsh. Nothing is dirty. The house smells nice, and there isn't any real garbage anywhere that I can see. It's just the toys. Endless piles of toys.

"Here we are. Pardon the mess but I am not the world's most organized person, as you may have already figured out. It's not all my mess, although most of it is. I mean, Chandra does have half the room, but she doesn't make half the mess. It's more like I make about two-thirds of the mess and she makes a quarter of it. No, that isn't right. What am I talking about? See, I told you I suck at math. Chandra would make a third. No, not that much. I guess I make three-quarters and she makes one. Or something like that. Anyway, I get in trouble a lot for being such a pig. I end up having to clean my mess and Chandra's and do extra chores so that I'll remember to do a better job!"

While she talks, she's throwing clothes onto the floor to make spaces for us to sit. The room looks a lot like the living room, except that the ammunition for this war is clothes instead of toys. They're everywhere; on the floor, the desk, the bed, a chair or two…or at least I think they're chairs, but I can't be sure because I can't really see them through the clothes. It's wild. I'm not much into clothes. I have a few pairs of pants and some tops. Two pairs of shoes. A jacket. I travel light.

"There. Have a seat. Homework first or do you want to talk?" I never want to do homework, but I'm not sure what I have to talk about, either. Tough decision.

"I don't know. You decide." Trying to sound generous. I sit down on what turns out to be a chair. Just as I make contact, the door flies open and a kid about ten flies in. She might be eleven or twelve—or twenty-three, for that matter. I can never figure out how old kids are.

"Rhiannon, Mom says you have until about five, and then she needs help getting the salad done and it's your night for the table. She also says did your friend phone home to be sure they know where she is, and she also says you have to let me come in 'cause it's my room too."

"OK about the five and the table setting. I'll take care of the phoning and I don't believe you about the coming in because even though I know it's your room, I have a friend over and we need to do homework and I know Mom would have told you to give me some space." Rhiannon shakes her head and kind of pushes the kid out of the room. She looks a little annoyed for a second but shakes it off so fast, I'm not sure. She digs through the mess on her desk for a minute and comes up with a cordless phone.

"Here. You'd better call before they start to worry."

Worry? Who would worry about me? I have to call but not for that reason. I have to call so I won't be read the riot act when I get "home." I make the call and get Sandi on the line. She doesn't seem to care whether I come home for supper or not, which is what I expected, but she also tells me to have a nice time, which kind of surprises me.

"Done," I say, handing Rhiannon back the phone. She takes it and tosses it onto the bed, probably never to be seen again, and then she looks at me like she expects me to sing or dance or something.

"So, what should we talk about?" she asks. I don't know. I thought talking was her department.

"Whatever you want."

"Oh, OK. Well, let's see. This is my room and I obviously like clothes more than I should. Um, I already told you I like science, which explains all the geeky books." She points around the room. I didn't notice the books when I first came in, but now that she says it, I realize that the bottom half of all the piles I thought were just clothes are actually made up of books. I can't believe how many books she has. I've never owned a book unless I had to for school. Fewer packing boxes.

Rhiannon is looking at me again. My turn to talk. But I have nothing to say.

"Nice room."

"What's your room like at MacAvoy?" She talks about it like it's no big deal, which I guess is kind of nice. So many other kids I met in other schools seemed uncomfortable with my whole fostergirl gig. They didn't know what to say to me about where I lived or my family or all of those other things people talk about. It's usually a conversation killer. Then again, there probably isn't any such thing as a conversation killer with Rhiannon.

"It's OK. Not as nice as this. I used to share it, too." I flash on Charlene for just a second and almost wonder how she's doing.

"Oh, so you know what it's like! It can be nice to have the company, but I like my privacy sometimes too. I almost never have a room to myself. There were a few weeks last year between kids but that was it."

"Between kids?"

"Well, last year a little girl ended up going back to live with her grandmother. Her name is Suzanna and she's really sweet. She was only here in temporary care because her mom had died and no one in her family lived close enough to take her right off. So after she left there was a gap before Chandra came so I had a bit of time to myself. But Chandra is here now so I guess I have to share again unless Mom decides to give me the little room where Shelly is now, which might not be fair to her. When I go to university I am definitely getting a single room. Do you want to go to university?"

"Chandra isn't your sister?" I ignore the university question, hoping it will go away. I'm more likely to go live on the moon than go to university.

"Oh, no. I don't have any brothers and sisters. Not bio ones anyway. I am the only bio kid in the house. Mom had some problems when I was born and they said she couldn't have any more."

"So, all those kids?"

"Well, the little girls, Hillary and Marie, are still foster kids. We haven't had them very long. The other little guys, Toby and Freddie, just come here during the day. My parents are formally adopting Chandra soon and we adopted Adam a few years ago, but you haven't met him yet because he goes to a different school than us and it lets out later. And then there is Shelly who has lived here for about a year, but we couldn't adopt her because her parents wouldn't sign the papers, even though they don't actually want her with them. That's it."

"Your parents are foster parents?"

"Foster parents, adoptive parents, and bio parents. That's them. Mom loves kids and is kind of a professional mother. I know it's really old fashioned but she likes it. She's really strict but nice at the same time so kids mostly respect her, which makes it less than totally crazy, although it gets pretty crazy. Mom says that being a mom is the toughest and most important job around and it should be respected by everyone, including the government. She's writing some kind of proposal thing that says mothers should be recognized as professionals and that would encourage more women to stay home and raise their children. I mean, she's an actual professional already but I get her point. Personally, I admire her, but I want a different kind of job. What about you?"

What about me? I'm still knocked out by the size of her family and the fact that she's surrounded by fosterkids. Maybe she's trying to add me to the pack.

"I want a job. Soon."

"Oh yeah, how soon?"

"Like yesterday."

"Any reason you're in such a hurry?"

"I need a job so I can get my social worker to help me get emancipated." Why did I tell her that? It's none of her business. Besides, she probably has no idea what I'm talking about and I don't feel like explaining.

"You really want to live on your own? I think that might be kind of lonely. I mean, I'd definitely like my own room but not my own whole place. Maybe when I'm older but not yet. You aren't sixteen yet, are you?"

"I will be in December." So she does understand.

"You're kidding! Me too. Isn't that amazing!"

"Sure. Amazing."

"Yeah, I can tell you're thrilled," she laughs. "Well, it's four thirty so I guess we'd better get our work done. Mom said five. And when she says five, she means it." I hadn't thought her mom looked all that tough when I saw her downstairs, but I've never been good at the first-impression thing.

Mom. That Chandra kid said "mom" also. I totally thought she was Rhiannon's sister. I never called my pseudomoms anything but their first name. Except at the place I stayed at for a year. The pseudomom there made me call her Mrs. Sampson. Real homey.

Supper is noisy. Everyone's talking at once, which is good because it means I don't have to talk at all. I can just watch and listen. Rhiannon's mom isn't at all chatty like Rhiannon, but her dad likes to tell a story or two. He's one of those people who just kind of sends out sparks when they're in a room. Guess that's where Rhiannon gets it. The little kids spill stuff and eat with their mouths open and cry when no one pays enough attention to them. The mom spends her whole time cleaning kids up and calming kids down. It's kind of interesting to watch her. She reminds me of Sandi the way she controls everyone. Her voice is quiet, but there's this sharp edge to her words that cuts through all of the noise and slices it down into manageable pieces. I don't think I saw her actually eat anything. Why do people have kids anyway? Kids should be born when they're about thirteen. Old enough to take care of themselves.

"Thanks for coming, Sadie. It's always nice to have a new face at the table. Come again anytime." Rhiannon's mom smiles her smile at me as I get ready to go, and I accidentally smile back. Her smile is like her voice, soft, with just enough steel in it to make you pay attention.

"Thanks," I answer, because I can't think of anything else to say. I can't remember too many people thanking me for coming anywhere before. Mostly they thanked me for leaving. Ha ha. Funny Sadie.

"See you in school tomorrow, Sadie!" Rhiannon calls out to me as I head off toward the house where I am pretending to live.

I walk into the house a few minutes later, expecting it to seem super quiet after the rowdiness of Rhiannon's place. As I come into the front hall, one of the Ks, I think it's Krista, comes toward me. She looks kind of scared, and I wonder if she's misplaced the other K or something.

"You might not want to go up there," she whispers, pointing toward the ceiling. I can hear yelling and pounding and running feet. World War Four.

"You know what's going on?" I ask, even though I don't actually want to know.

"Buffy," she says, twirling her finger around next to her head in the universal sign for "crazy." Looking a bit crazy herself, she scuttles off to her room like a little crab. K Number Two is probably already burrowed down in there for the night. At least they have each other.

I look up at the ceiling again. It's still making a lot of noise. I don't really want to go up, but I don't want to sit down here either. Maybe I could sneak by and make it into my room without anyone noticing me. It sounds like they're busy anyway.

I walk carefully up the stairs and into the hall, where my plans to hide are blown away. The war is taking place in the upstairs hallway, right in front of my room. I can't really retreat because Alisha has already seen me.

"Sadie, get this idiot off me!" She pulls one of her arms loose from the hold that the worker has on her. It's one of the part-timers, Sarah, I think, and she's struggling to get a better grip. They look like badly paid pro wrestlers as they crash to the floor.

"Sarah!" Sandi says. She's got Buffy in one of those special holds, the kind they learn in self-defense class or wherever it is that the grouphome and fosterhome workers get trained to "control" kids who can't control themselves. I've never been held like that, being the passive type, but I've seen it lots of times and it has never looked like fun. For anyone. Sometimes it looks kind of funny, though, like right now, with Alisha on the floor sitting on top of Sarah, who just looks stupid as she lies there holding on to Alisha.

"Sarah, enough. She's probably OK." Sandi is obviously the boss and the other worker bees always do what she says. Sarah lets go, and Alisha gets up.

"You don't need to do that. I'm only defending myself. Man, don't you know when to use that stuff? Sandi, you need to teach this girl here a thing or two!" Alisha brushes herself off and looks at Sarah like she's a tiny little worm that she wants to squish. Sandi looks at her kind of the same way. I have a feeling she's going to be giving her a "talk" later. The thought warms my heart a little. Sarah just looks messed up, pissed off, and a little embarrassed.

"Alisha, enough. Sarah, go check on the little ones. Buffy, you've get to try to calm down, kiddo." Sandi says all of this in a calm voice while holding on to Buffy, who is kicking and spitting and basically having a total freakazoid fit.

"Kiddo needs to seriously chill and to shut her stupid mouth," Alisha says, sending Buffy into total whacked out slayer mode. I think I even heard her growl.

"Alisha, enough. You and Sadie both go into her room. Buffy and I need some quiet time." When Sandi talks, even Alisha usually listens. We both go into my room. As I close the door, I can hear Sandi talking quietly and Buffy starting to cry. It will be over soon. Usually when they cry, it means they're ready to stop kicking.

"What happened?" I ask, not that I care.

"She's just nuts. Came home all bummed about something at school and started taking it out on me. I said a few things. Guess they were the wrong things. She gets mad and comes at me, scratching with her little cat claws. Guess she's trying to slay me." She grins.

"Which I'm sure you said to her just to make things so much better."

"Maybe. Anyway, she's on top of me all screaming and scratching, and Sarah comes out of nowhere and grabs me. Like she's on the slayer's side and is holding me so she can get her fangs into me too."

"I thought the vamps have fangs, not the Buffy."

"Whatever. Anyway, I start yelling at Sarah, and Buffy's screaming at me, and then Sandi comes in and grabs Buffy, and then everyone is having a party."

"Sorry I missed most of it."

"Yeah, well, Sandi's going to set that brain-dead halfwit straight, anyway. Grabbing me when I'm perfectly calm and in control!"

"Imagine." I shake my head and she laughs.

"Anyway, I can't stand rooming with Buffy any more. She's whacked. And if she doesn't stop being such a nut job someone is going to actually whack her. If I don't get out of there, it might be me." She looks at me kind of like Rhiannon did in her room. Expecting me to do something. Only, this time, I know what Alisha wants. My privacy. I don't want a roommate. Charlene never came back from the hospital, and that's just fine with me. Guess they figured her out after all. Not sure where she ended up, but I bet it's somewhere more secure than here where she won't be able to find nice sharp decorating tools. But I figure it will only be a matter of time before Sandi finds some other reject to sleep in Charlene's ex-bed, so it might as well be Alisha. What's that stupid expression that Mrs. Sampson used to use? Oh, yeah. Better the devil you know.

"OK, you can move in," I say, even though it's not OK at all. It sucks that I'm being punished for their sins. There, I think about Sampson and I start talking like Sunday school. She used to make me go to Sunday school. Said it would wash away my sins and make me pure. I was only about ten at the time. How many sins could I have had?

So, Alisha has moved in. It's an improvement over Charlene, but not by much. Charlene moaned and groaned and hurt herself. Alisha snores and talks about all of the wonderful ways she's going to hurt everyone else. She also talks nonstop about her mother and how she's drying out and getting ready for her to come home.

"Except now I probably can't go home this weekend. My zit-faced social witch might hear about the thing with Buffy and decide I'm not stable enough. Maybe Sandi will stand up for me and tell her it's stupid Sarah's fault. She needs to seriously fire her ass. People like that should work with dogs, not kids. Scratch that. She's too stupid to work with dogs. Anyway, my mom will be majorly disappointed if I don't come home. She's been working really hard to stay clean and sober and all. She even has a job interview so she can say that she can support me. If Buffy baby messed up my weekend, she's in for a world of hurt."

I drift off to sleep as she snarls away. She talks as much as Rhiannon does, but somehow Rhiannon's babbling makes me feel kind of light, like the world isn't quite so disgusting for a minute or two. Alisha just makes me feel like turning off the light and keeping my eyes shut for a long, long time.

chapter 8

Friday afternoon and I have a pink slip that says I have to go see Jackson in the guidance office. I can't think of anything I want to do less. I don't want to be stuck in this hole one second longer than I have to. I even have plans for after school. I'm going to Rhiannon's to watch movies. Not that it sounds very exciting and I'm not thrilled at the idea of being stuck in the middle of the scary rugrats, but it's better than going to MacAvoy House and listening to Alisha complain about being stuck at the house instead of going home to her saintly mother.

I get down to the office and I'm just about to walk in when I hear more than one person talking. I don't want to face two teachers at two thirty on a Friday afternoon, so I sit down and hope they shut up soon. Since I don't have anything better to do, I listen to what they're saying. Not that I'm interested, but they aren't exactly being quiet.

"I don't think it's a valid referral, Nancy."

"Why not? As if I don't already know." That's Jackson's voice. I'm not sure who the other one is.

"Don't start with that. We have to be realistic. We don't get all that many kids through each year and we have to focus on the ones we think we can actually do something with."

"And why would you assume that we can't do anything with Sadie?" Sadie? That perks up my ears.

"It's the same for all of those group home girls. They've been to so many schools that it isn't any wonder they have trouble learning. It's a stretch to go looking for some sort of learning disability when there are so many other factors." Learning disability? What the hell is that? Do they think I'm retarded or something? Typical. Jackson acts like she's on my side and all the time she's trying to add to my labels.

"Just because she's had a rough life doesn't mean there isn't something else going on. If there is, it can make a big difference to her to know. You know that!"

"I do know that. I also know that girls from MacAvoy house aren't usually here for even a full year, let alone long enough for us to actually test them and then do something about it."

Test me? Are they kidding? I'm not doing any stupid tests. Had enough of that in the hospital when I was little. Didn't cure me then and won't cure me now.

"It's still only September, and we have spots. If we put the paper work in next week, Steven might be able to come in next month. I called him and asked, and he's not swamped yet. But he will be if we wait any longer."

Good, wait then.

"So, we do the testing, get the results by, say, Christmas, and then she disappears in January. Then we've wasted a spot."

"Wasted? It would still help her to know. The results can go to her next school if she leaves. There's something about her that just makes me think we can do something different for her. She needs something!"

Jackson sounds upset. Well, she can join the club.

"I don't need anything!" I walk into the office without knocking. I figure if they can talk about me behind my back, I can break a few manners myself. "Actually, I take that back. I do need something. I need people to get out of my face and out of my life. Just for the record, I am not retarded. I just hate school. It's stupid, and so I look stupid when I'm here. No one thinks I'm stupid outside." I'm thoroughly pissed, but I shock myself when I feel tears pop into my eyes. Maybe I am stupid everywhere. Only a stupid person would cry because some backstabbing teacher does what all teachers do.

"I don't think you're stupid at all, Sadie!" Jackson says, sounding even more upset. The other teacher, who I don't even know, shakes her head and walks out of the room. Who is she to be talking about me at all! Not that Jackson has any right to be chatting about my life, either.

"Of course you do. I heard you. I might be stupid but I'm not deaf. Man, I was actually letting myself start to think you were kind of different, you know? Like you give a crap. Obviously, I am totally stupid or I wouldn't have been sucked in by your whole I-want-to-help routine."

"I do want to help and it's not a routine. Could you sit down a minute and let me explain?" Her voice is calm now. I don't want to sit down, but I don't want to get in trouble, either. I've been keeping it clean. I even did a couple of English assignments… with a little help from the fact that Rhiannon already passed the course and still has her notes, which she somehow found in her room under a pile of clothes and science books.

"Fine." Except that it isn't.

"I'm sorry. This isn't at all how I wanted to do this. I hadn't expected Ms. Williams to be here when you got here."

"So, you're just sorry that I heard you talking behind my back."

"Touché. I am sorry that I didn't talk to you first and let you know what I've been thinking. I'm treating you like a little girl. I realize that you aren't. You're pretty mature for your age."

"Whatever that means."

"I guess it just means that you've been through a lot and it's made you a little wiser about the world."

"Wise and stupid at the same time."

"You have to stop with that word, Sadie."

"Why?"

"Well, for starters, I hate that word. I don't think it describes anyone. And I've talked to you and watched you, Sadie. I know there's a good mind in that head of yours. I just think that maybe the way schools want you to show us what you know isn't the way that works for you."

"What?" She's talking in circles.

"Not everyone learns the same way, but schools have a habit of teaching everyone as if they did. That's starting to change in lots of ways, but we aren't all the way there yet. Kids who have trouble with visual tasks like reading and writing have trouble in school."

"That seems kind of obvious."

"It might be obvious to you! Most things we do in school involve putting things down on paper and getting things off of it. But there are lots of kids out there who understand concepts and know what's going on, but can't express themselves in writing and have trouble deciphering words in print." I know where this is heading, and I don't think I like it.

"So, what's that got to do with me?"

"I would just like to do a few little tests with you to see if there might be something going on that might be getting in your way. Find out if there are other ways we could teach you to tell us what you know."

"I can read and write. I just don't like to bother with it." It sounds like a lie. It isn't really a total lie. I can read. Some. Just really slowly and nothing too complicated. Makes me feel stupid. I can understand stuff when someone reads it out loud or whatever, but it gets all messed up if I read it myself. I always figured I was sleeping when they taught reading in grade one. I can't remember. Maybe that's it. I learned it but I have such a pathetic memory that I can't keep it in my empty head.

"I know you can. But it's not exactly easy for you, is it?" I debate lying again, but since it didn't work the first time I give up.

"No, but I don't try very hard either."

"Well, when something is that hard, most people stop trying after a while. It's like me and music. I love listening to people sing and always wanted to do it. But I seem to be tone deaf, and no matter how hard I try, my voice sounds awful. The difference is, the thing I have trouble with wasn't the thing that everyone in school wanted me to do. No one really cared that I couldn't sing, except maybe the choir teacher. It's so much tougher when the thing you have trouble with is reading or writing…at least when you're in school, where it's considered so important."

I'm listening but I'm not hearing anything too helpful. "So, you do these tests and they say I can't read or write properly. We already know that, so why bother?"

"Reading and writing are both more than just deciphering symbols. Reading can be about understanding what you hear, not just what you see. Writing can be about what you say, not what you put down on paper. There are lots of neat things we can teach you that could help you show us what you can do. Which I will do with or without the testing, but I'd still like to try the testing just to help us understand you better."

"I understand me fine. I don't think I want to know any more right now."

"All right. If you change your mind, come and see me."

"That other lady says I'm not worth the effort." I don't know why I say that. Why do I care?

"She didn't really mean that. It's just that we don't have the time or resources to test a lot of kids, and girls in your situation sometimes leave in the middle of the year. I don't think that should be a deciding factor, though."

"Yeah, I heard. I guess maybe you were kind of sticking up for me?"

"Well, I guess so. Not that Ms. Williams is against you in any way."

"Sure."

"I am sure about that. Anyway, I'll let you head off. I would still like to spend a little time with you trying a few things that might make school a little less dreadful. How do you feel about that?"

"I don't know. I guess so. Maybe."

"OK, I guess that's the best I'm getting right now. Have a good weekend, Sadie." She smiles at me. I don't really smile back, but I don't spit at her either.

I can't really figure Jackson out. She seems all supportive and everything, getting Wilson to back off and even standing up for me with that Williams chick. But this testing bit confuses things. I can't figure out if that means she's on my side or not. Last time anyone talked to me about testing was in the hospital and they were trying to force me to do something I didn't want to do. They tested me, labeled me, and cut me loose. Didn't help.

Why would I want to go through that garbage again?

"I don't think she'd suggest it if it's a bad idea, Sadie. Jackson is pretty cool compared to most teachers. I mean, there are a few really nice teachers in our school but I think she's the smartest and nicest at the same time, which is a good combination. She really cares about kids, you know? I think you should do what she says. I mean, I know you're really smart. Maybe the tests will prove it." Rhiannon always has an opinion. Which I guess is the reason I tell her about the meeting with Jackson. I'm not used to talking to people about stuff that happens to me, so I'm surprised when my mouth opens and all this personal information comes spewing out at Rhiannon on the way to her house. I guess she's just in the wrong place at the wrong time.

"I don't know. Sounds all pretty bogus to me. I mean, I know I'm the world's crappiest student and all, but I don't think it's from any fancy learning disability or whatever. I'm not even sure what a learning disability is except that it's one more thing wrong with me." Man, I have verbal diarrhea today. I can't shut up.

"There's nothing wrong with you. At least no more than there is with me. I talk too much and the teachers think I have ADHD. You don't talk very much at all. I read too much when I'm supposed to be doing other things. You listen instead of reading and the teachers think you might have an LD. I am a total pig. You are totally clean. Actually, when you think of it, there's more wrong with me than with you!"

She laughs at herself. I shake my head at her, but I feel myself smiling while I do it. She's a total nut job.

I try to put the whole testing idea out of my mind for the rest of the evening so I can try to enjoy another noisy night in the Rhiannon house. Movies turn out to be a whole-family affair, with everyone crammed into a slightly cleaned up living room. That means we have to watch G-rated videos, which I haven't done since…well, maybe never. It's some animated thing about a rat who cooks, which seems kind of lame to me, but makes everyone laugh their heads off. The little kids are slightly less scary in their pyjamas sitting on the couch with Rhiannon's parents, all curled up like little rag dolls or something, with their thumbs stuck in their mouths plugging up the holes so that there isn't any scream-ing. Chandra and Shelly are both home and lying on the floor on either side of Adam, who laughs harder than anyone.

Adam's what people call "special needs." I can't tell what makes his needs so special, but he sure is different than any guy I ever knew. He's big and that could have been scary, but he has these really gentle eyes. He doesn't seem super slow or anything, but he doesn't really look directly at you, and he always seems to talk to someone behind you when he's supposed to be talking to you. He walks around in a bit of a daze, like there is always some fog in his way. He loves movies and computers, though, and seems to sort of wake up a bit whenever he is around either of them. I think it's odd that Rhiannon's folks have adopted him. I mean, he is sweet and all, but he's probably lots of work. Maybe they didn't know he was so special when they picked him?

Thinking about Adam distracts me from the movie and turns

my head back to Jackson and her testing crap. Does she want me to be "special needs," too? If I come out special will I be sent to another school like Adam? A school for special fostergirls who can't read worth crap and couldn't write an essay even if you stood over them with a knife?

Maybe I should go to cooking school instead. If a rat can do it, I probably can, too.

chapter 9

A week later, and I feel even more like a rat. Trapped in a maze disguised as a closet disguised as a testing room, with Jackson playing the role of mad scientist. Not sure why I agreed to this. Mostly to shut everyone up.

I'm sweating in here, probably starting to smell bad like I'm rotting from the inside out. Serves Jackson right for making me do this.

"OK, Sadie, I'm going to read you some number sequences. I would like you to repeat them exactly as you hear them. Remember, they're supposed to be hard, so don't worry if you have trouble."

Easy for her to say. She knows the way out of the maze.

I'm staring at a blank wall that doesn't have any answers for me.

"Auditory processing," Jackson explains, even though I haven't asked. "It doesn't measure whether or not you can actually hear. It helps to measure whether or not you can process what you hear.

Do the messages come in clearly, or do they get scrambled a little in translation."

Lots of messages get scrambled in my world, but that isn't because *I* have a problem listening. It's because the so-called adults in my life have problems communicating. Maybe Jackson should test them.

I sit there repeating numbers to her, probably all in the wrong order. Then she switches to words, which don't have to be in the right order. This I can do. Then she revs it up to full sentences which start out OK, but then start to sound like Rhiannon, they're so long. This I cannot do. I'm already tired of this. They should put a TV in front of me instead of a blank wall. I can watch TV just fine. So long as there isn't a quiz after the show.

"Visual processing," Jackson explains as we enter Phase Two of the torture session, even though I still don't ask. Assessing whether my eyes can process what they see. Do the signals get to my brain the way they're supposed to, or do they get totally screwed up on the way.

I have to look at rows of little pictures that disappear from my brain two seconds after I try to put them in. They aren't getting scrambled. They don't even make it into the frying pan.

Phase Three and it only gets worse.

"I'm going to give you some words, and I just want you to read them one at a time. Don't rush it and don't worry if you have trouble. Just sound them out as best you can and move on."

Doesn't she remember how we met in the first place?

"You want me to read? Out loud?"

"I know you hate reading. I need you to do this part. It's only one word at a time and no one else can hear you."

The words are all sitting in a row, mocking me and daring me to call them by name. I manage the first few but the sweat gets into my eyes and I can't read the rest.

"That's OK. We'll move on."

It's not really OK.

Phase Four and I start to see a little light. Numbers and equations have always been much friendlier than letters and words. They don't make fun of me. Especially when Jackson reads all of the questions to me, and I answer without a pencil.

Phase Five and I'm totally lost again. More words on the page, but this time there are whole paragraphs. The words swirl around and trip over each other, jumping from line to line, laughing at me when I try to get them to stay still. Jackson asks questions that have no answers.

The rat loses.

"OK, just a couple more sections. You're doing great." Such a nice lie. She's not even looking at me when she says it. If she was, she'd notice that I'm melting away into a puddle in the chair. Maybe she doesn't care. She'll just mop me up and move on to the next kid.

Phase Six. Stories on a CD with questions I can answer without writing. The reader's voice draws pictures in my mind that stay with me long enough to give Jackson an answer or two before I start to melt again.

Last, and most definitely least, I am handed a pencil and asked to write my way out. This I cannot do. I guess I will be trapped in here forever.

"OK, we're done. You look a little done in." My captor takes pity on me and takes away my pencil, which I give up willingly.

"Yeah. Room's kind of small and hot." Not to mention the instruments of torture she has been tormenting me with.

"I know. I spend a lot of time in here."

"Doing what?"

"What I'm doing right now with you."

"You test that many kids?" Somehow, I thought I was the only one.

"I do. This is a big school, even though the town is small. We bring kids in from all over the county. There are lots of kids who manage to get through to high school without recognizing their learning problems."

"Yeah, figures. Lots of crappy teachers out there." I figured she would be ticked with that one. She surprises me by half-smiling and shaking her head.

"It's too bad you feel that way. I can't lie and say that everyone who teaches does a great job. Lots do, though. There are other reasons kids slip through." Slip through? She makes it sound like something easy, like tubing down a water slide. I sure didn't slip through school. It's more like being shoved through, kicking and screaming and begging for mercy.

She thanks me for coming, as if we have just had a tea party or something. I think I even say "you're welcome," which is a total lie, because she isn't welcome at all. I would be happy if I never saw her or her lame brain tests again. It's only going to prove what I've always known.

When it comes to the real world, my brain does me just fine. When it comes to reading and writing at school, my brain is basically useless. Put a pen in my hand and nothing comes out the end of it. I can't think of anything to say, and even if a miracle happens and a thought does creep into my mind, I can't get it to go down on the paper the same way it came into my head. By the time I finish making a mess of Thought One, any other thoughts have gone screaming away into the night.

Reading. I don't know what the deal is with that. I probably didn't pay any attention back in baby school and that's why the words are so hard to figure out. I mean, I can read. Everyone can read. There's lots of words I recognize 'cause I've seen them a million times. But you put a whole page of those suckers in front of me and they all seem to blend together and do a happy dance across the page. I can't see where one ends and the next one starts, and it takes me forever to figure it all out. Which might just mean I am stupid, in spite of what Jackson says. It also means *I do not read out loud*. Wilsons of the world take note.

I head home at the end of the day, just late enough that Rhiannon actually gave up and left without me. I thought I'd be glad for the silence, seeing as I feel like I've been beaten over the head with a baseball bat for four hours or so.

The weird thing is, I kind of wish she was here so I could tell her about the testing and hear her talk for forty-five minutes about how awesome it sounded and how she wished she could have testing and how wonderful she thinks I did and how great Jackson is and how super our school is and...

Just weird.

chapter 10

Weekends at MacAvoy basically suck. But that isn't surprising, because everything at MacAvoy basically sucks. Alisha's gums flapping all of the time, and Buffy skulking around looking for someone to get in trouble. She doesn't have a new roommate yet, so she has too much time on her hands. She always seems to be standing outside my door when I leave my room to go to the bathroom or something else equally exciting. On the other hand, the Ks are basically invisible. They hole up in their room like little field mice most of the time. When they do come out, they don't talk to us much. They just look kind of scared if we look at them. Alisha likes to glare at them and give them the finger behind the workers' backs. She thinks it's funny. I don't think it's funny. I think it's stupid.

Sometimes we go out places, which sucks even more than staying in the house. There's nothing more pathetic than five loser group home girls wandering around together with their worker tagging along like a demented hen chasing her chicks. We're so obviously nut jobs that everyone stares at us anywhere we go. Alisha and Buffy stare back and make loud and obnoxious comments that make the hen even more demented. The Ks ignore them and just kind of blend together into one slightly bigger K. I ignore everyone and try to look like I'm by myself.

This Saturday we've all been herded into the van and taken off to the video store to choose movies. That is our big outing for the weekend. Of all the lame things we do, this is the lamest. We have to pick three movies between the five of us, and the movies have to be OK for all of us.

"Are you freakin' kidding me? I'm not watching that baby crap!" Alisha is shouting at one of the Ks.

"Alisha!" The hen of the night looks up from the other aisle, twitching a little as she pokes her beak over the rows of well-behaved DVDs.

"Come on! Seriously, I'm not twelve. I'm not watching G movies!"

"Come on, Alisha. The Ks are just little kids. They have to watch G movies. Right, guys?" Buffy smiles at the Ks and they actually smile back and kind of creep over to stand behind her, like she's going to protect them from Alisha or something. Crazy. Don't they know Buffy is out of her little mind? Alisha does not smile. She looks at Buffy like she's going to feed her a DVD sandwich. The hen doesn't seem to notice and just keeps clucking.

"You get three movies. One can be for the younger girls. You three older girls can decide on the other two. Nothing more than PG, though."

"Oh, goody. We girls will get right on that. Here, how about this one. *Sexy Sirens*." Alisha wanders to another aisle and is waving a movie at us.

"How can a siren be sexy? Isn't it just noisy?" Buffy asks. Alisha laughs.

"You are such a total idiot! Why don't you head back over to the baby section with your little babies!" she says just loudly enough so that everyone in the next town can hear her. Buffy throws the DVD case she's holding at her. The Ks hold hands and shift away from Buffy to find a new safe spot. Buffy doesn't notice, because she's too busy glaring at Alisha. I think her switch has flipped from protector to killer. Maybe I should go and hide out with the Ks.

"Girls!" The hen, whose name is Allison, I think, scuttles over to save the day.

"What's your problem?" Alisha has Buffy by the front of her shirt, shaking her. The hen is pecking at them, trying to separate them, but Alisha has a pretty good grip. Buffy looks like she's trying to scratch Alisha's eyes out again. I just watch the action, wondering where the nearest exit is so I can make my escape.

"Sadie! I can't believe you're here! I just finished asking my mom if you can come over tomorrow and she said sure. I'm here with Chandra and Mom picking movies for the gang. I didn't see you at first because we're over in the Family section. Although, we are going to pick a couple for after the little ones go to bed. Maybe you could come over tonight instead?" Rhiannon stops for breath, smiling at everyone. She doesn't seem to notice that Alisha is about to throw Buffy through the window and that there's a hen flapping her useless wings trying to stop her. Everyone just morphs into a bunch of bizarre-looking mannequins, frozen in place as they all stare at Rhiannon like she's some kind of alien who just fell out of her spaceship through the ceiling of the video store. She doesn't notice that, either.

"Hi. I'm Rhiannon," she says, stepping forward and looking at Allison as if she wants to shake hands or something. Alisha kind of snarls at her.

"They don't care who you are. Take off!" She lets go of Buffy and steps toward Rhiannon as if she's going to grab her. Rhiannon's smile kind of falls off her face, and she looks at me as she steps back out of range.

"Back off, Alisha." I can't believe my mouth let the words out. I don't get involved in stupid arguments.

"Back off? You're telling me to back off your little friend? Did I scare her with my big bad mouth?"

"Just leave it, OK?" My mouth seems to be stuck open with words coming out.

"You're that kid who lives in that foster home, right? Your mom has like a million foster kids all the time. You a foster kid, too?"

"No. You know that." Rhiannon's voice is quiet and she's looking down at the floor, like she's trying to avoid Alisha's eyes. Don't blame her. They're probably registered somewhere as lethal weapons.

"Oh, yeah, I forgot. So you're like a professional foster sister or whatever. Taking pity on all the poor little foster kids like your mommy does. That's why you hang with poor little Sadie here, right? Just another foster girl to add to your collection?" She smiles at me when she says it. I don't smile back. I want to punch her in the face, but I don't do it. Don't want to make a bigger scene than we're already making.

"We're going. Now! Don't make me call." Allison is standing pointing toward the door. *Don't make me call* is every worker's favorite threat. Calling means getting Sandi away from wherever she is and making her come and save the day. This seriously pisses Sandi off when it happens and she finds quiet little ways of making our already hellish lives go even deeper down the hole. She's not too easy on the hen of the night, either. Probably sends her back to the coop for retraining.

"Fine. See you later, foster sister." Alisha walks past Rhiannon and kind of brushes against her, knocking her back into the videos. The Ks have already scurried out to the van, and Buffy is stomping out behind Allison. Rhiannon looks at me like she's expecting me to say or do something. I just stand there. Her eyes look kind of wet, like maybe she's thinking of crying. I really hope she doesn't. I hate crying. Besides, Alisha's not worth even one tear.

"Uh, I guess I'd better get back to my mom," Rhiannon says.

"Yeah."

"Sadie, about what your friend says…"

"She's not my friend and I don't listen to what she says!" My words fly out harder than I expected and slap her in the face. I don't think Rhiannon has ever heard me yell before, and she flinches a little.

"Oh. OK. Good. I'll call you about coming over." She tries a smile, but it's dull and flickering, a lightbulb about to go out.

"I think I'm busy all weekend." Not sure where that's coming from. It's not even true.

"Oh. OK. Well. Another time." Her voice is still quiet and her eyes drop back down to the floor. Maybe there's something interesting written on it. I resist the urge to check. I have a feeling that she's upset and that I'm supposed to do something about that. I can't think of anything and, besides, I'm not too thrilled about being part of the freak show, either.

I walk to the van and get in. I don't look at anyone or talk to anyone. Allison must have told them all to keep their lips together because no one else talks either. The ride home is short and quiet. When we get home, there is nothing to do because we left without the movies. I don't care. I don't want to watch movies with them anyway.

I don't want to go to my room because Alisha is in there, and I don't want to hear any more of her mouth. Not that I listen to her. At least I try not to.

I go out back and sit on the step. I try not to think about Alisha's big mouth but her words seemed to have stuck themselves in my brain. Figures. Can't get anything useful to stay in my mind for long, but her words manage to find a place to sit.

I wonder about what she says. It would explain a lot. I mean, I'm not exactly the kind of person that people hook themselves on to. I had a few so-called friends I hung with a bit in my last couple of schools, but it wasn't any big deal. I never went home with them to meet their mommies or anything. I never brought them home to meet my pseudoparents, either. We just kind of hung out together when there was nothing better to do.

This Rhiannon babe is different. She asks me questions about myself and tells me things about herself. She wants me to spend time with her family. She attached herself to me from Day One. I never could figure out why. I thought maybe she was just too lazy to look around for someone better.

But Alisha's version makes more sense. Why else would a kid like her want to hang with someone like me? She's used to the whole foster deal. Her mom's done the fostering thing her whole life and probably told her that she has to be nice to the poor pathetic group home girls because no one else likes them. She picked me because I'm new and probably because Alisha and Buffy are both scarier than me. They're both aggressive, without the passive.

Man, what an idiot. I have actually been going over to that house and eating supper with all those dweeby kids and thinking…I don't know what. That's the problem. I haven't been thinking. Stupid, stupid Sadie. Wasting my time. Not that I have much to do with my time, but there has to be something better than making a fool out of myself.

It starts to rain on top of me, not that sprinkly kind that you can sit in, but big buckets of water dumping on my head. I run inside and stand for a second or two deciding where to go next. I walk into the main room, where the Ks are sitting on the couch watching a movie about cheerleaders who look like hookers. I wondered if it's G rated. Not that I care. They ignore me and I ignore them back. I head up to my room because I can't think of anywhere else to go.

"Hey," Alisha says as I walk through the door. She's lying on her bed doing nothing. Her favorite activity. I ignore her and go over to my own side of the room. Not that there're really two sides. The room reminds me of the closet Jackson uses, except that this one has a window. I could lie in bed and reach out and smack Alisha on the nose when she snores. Not that I do that, being passive and all.

"Come on! You're not pissed 'cause of what I said to that little nerd kid, are you? I mean, I'm just telling you the truth. Didn't think it would, like, upset you or whatever." She doesn't look too sorry. Just kind of annoyed that I'm not happy to see her. Don't know why. I have never ever acted happy to see her.

"Nothing you do could upset me. That would mean I care." I flop down on my bed and put my arms over my eyes, hoping Alisha will take the hint.

"That Rhiannon kid is a total freak, anyway. I've been here longer than you. I know the score around here. She's more of a reject than we are. None of the kids hang around her. She's always babbling and acting weird. She had one other totally freakazoid friend when I first came here, but I think the kid got beamed back up to her spaceship or something." She laughs at herself. I don't move or answer.

"Hey, you alive over there? I know you're not sleeping."

"Shut up, Alisha."

"Shut up? You tell *me* to shut up? Girl, you have no idea who your friends really are. You need to stick to your own kind. Those kids at that stuck-up school don't understand us. They're all a bunch of baby-faced sucks with mommies who still wipe their bums. They know nothing. They look at us like we're scum. They're the ones who're scum."

"You still have a mom." My stupid mouth opened without permission again.

"Yeah, but she don't wipe no bums! My mom's cool. She treats me like a grownup. Always did. That's part of why I'm in this garbage heap. The stupid teachers at one of my schools found out my mom and I were drinking together. They called the cops or whoever, and there was a big investigation. They said all kinds of lies, like she gave me drugs and was sleeping with guys for money in front of me. Lies. It's just a drink. She's just respecting me."

"Sure."

"It's true. She doesn't think kids should be treated different from adults. She always talks to me like a real grownup. She doesn't hide nothing from me. She's so much cooler than the babes who hang out here. I can't wait to get home."

"Why're you here?"

"You mean now? On a Saturday? I don't know. Some lies about her not showing up at her AA meeting or whatever. There's all these conditions on me visiting. It's so bogus. She's my mom. They have no right to keep me away from her."

"Guess not."

"Damn right. One of these days, I'm going to figure out a plan to split this place and get my mom to take me away where no one can find us. We can just be ourselves again."

"Who are you now?"

"I have no freakin' idea."

She finally stops talking and seems to either fall asleep or slip into a coma. Either way, her breathing is steady and her mouth is closed. I can't sleep. I have no idea if it's anywhere near a time when I would want to be asleep. It doesn't matter. My stupid head seems to be swirling around with other people's words, keeping me awake and hurting my brain.

At least Alisha has a mother. Someone she figures wants her around. I don't know if I have one or not. I'm allowed to know, but I never ask. It's bad enough knowing that all of my pseudomothers don't want me around. Don't need to know my so-called real one hated me, too.

chapter 11

I spent Sunday wandering around town and thinking about nothing and found a different route to school that basically heads the opposite way from my usual. It seems like a more practical route to me, so I take it on Monday morning. It's a quieter walk than usual.

I see Rhiannon for a second when I get to school. She's running across the front lawn, late as usual. I'm already at the door and decide not to wait. I can't think of anything to say to her, anyway. Not that she would care because she can always find lots to say. I'm not in the mood to listen, though.

First class, I get one of those stupid pink slips inviting me to talk to Jackson. I don't want to talk to Jackson again so soon. I just spent most of Friday with her and figure that's enough for this lifetime. But the trouble with those pink slips is they don't come with an "I don't want to see you" option.

"Sadie, I scored your testing over the weekend," Jackson says when I force myself down there at lunchtime. It's better than trying to avoid people in the cafeteria, anyway.

"Yeah." Her weekend sounds even more pathetic than mine, if that's possible.

"Yeah. And I have some ideas of things we can try to see if we can make things a little better for you at school. I also have some papers I need your guardian to sign."

"Papers?" Guardian means Cecilia, who would just use this as another excuse to keep me in MacAvoy until I'm twenty-five.

"Just a permission form for the psychometrist to come and do a bit more testing. I think we need to find out more about what is going on with you." She looks kind of pleased with herself, like she's offering me a trip to Vegas.

"I've already been tested by shrinks. You probably already know that 'cause I figure you read my file already."

"Not a shrink, Sadie. The school board psychometrist is only interested in how you learn. The tests all focus on that. It's not much different from what we already did, although some kids find it easier." Still doesn't sound like a trip to Vegas to me.

"Don't think so. My guardian is hard to get hold of anyway. I only see her once a month or whatever. No more tests." I'm tired. My brain hurts.

"Can you think about it at least?" she asks.

"I don't need to this time. I'm not interested. I did enough."

"OK. Well, we'll just go with what we have then. I'd like to go over these test results with you a bit and then explain what we can do about it." She has the booklet things she had been writing in while putting me through her little four-hour torture session. She looks at them like they're interesting, which I'm sure they're not.

"Whatever." I don't want to hear it, but I don't want to get into a hassle with her over it, either. I figure she can talk and I can pretend to listen and just put my mind to sleep.

"OK. These results aren't conclusive or anything. They just measure how you're doing in different areas, but they don't tell us why. That's why I wanted the psychometrist to come...anyway. Never mind about that. This first one, remember, the auditory test where you have to stare at the wall?" I nod. Obviously I remember. It's only been two days. Does she think I'm totally stupid? Maybe. Maybe that's what's coming next.

"Your scores were quite strong across the board on this one. They seem to indicate that you do very well when you're using listening as your learning method."

I try not to laugh out loud. Listening! I do everything I can not to listen in school! I'm not sure why I'm listening to her right now!

"My ears are fine."

"I know. You told me. And, as I told you, it's not about that so much as what your brain does with the information that gets in through your ears. Yours seem to process it quite well. This test shows a somewhat different pattern, though." She puts the other one, the one with all the dumb symbols and things, in front of me. "It shows some highs and lows, but overall is lower than the auditory results. It seems from this that your visual learning skills are somewhat weaker than your auditory."

"Sure, whatever."

"I can tell you're fascinated. It does matter, though. When you were little, you were mostly taught to use visual skills...reading books, reading off the board, writing things down, reading silently, reading math problems to yourself.... Well, the list is endless. Kids who have some difficulties with visual processing can find school really tough."

"I'm pretty sure I wasn't paying much attention when they taught all that stuff. I never liked school much."

"Well, that's kind of a chicken-and-egg type thing."

"Chicken and egg?" We're talking food now?

"Which came first? Did you hate school because it's hard or is it hard because you hated it? Doesn't matter anymore. You are here now and we have some data that can help us help you."

Who is the "us" she's talking about?

"I still hate school."

"I'm not surprised. School doesn't really fit your learning style all that well. And moving around all the time didn't help you or your teachers figure you out."

"I can't read worth crap." Not only is my brain refusing to cooperate and sleep, now my mouth is spouting things I don't want spouted.

"I know. Part of reading is based on visual processing. Not all of it, but a lot of it. If you can't process the symbols comfortably, it's hard to get the meaning out of the words. There is a huge difference on this test between what you could understand when you heard the stories on the CD and when you had to read on your own."

"Yeah, well that doesn't help much. School books aren't on CD."

"That's the kind of cool thing. Lots of them are."

"Doesn't sound like a bestseller." She laughs as if I'm making a lame joke.

"You'd be surprised. Lots of schools use them. Even better, we have computer programs that can read books on CDs to you. You can even scan books onto the hard drive, so you can read anything that is in print or even on the Internet."

"So everyone can laugh at me." Sounds like fun.

"Not everyone. Some people might be ignorant enough to bother you about it. But there are ways to minimize that. There are computers all over the school. We have headphones so that no one can hear what you're hearing. You can work at the back of the class or in the resource room."

"The sped room? You have to be kidding me!" Every school has one. The special ed room where all the dumb kids hang out.

"Lots of kids use the resource room. It's used for all sorts of things. People who've been sick and need to catch up, kids in the university prep course who want a quiet space, kids who just need a little extra help from time to time."

"And the speds. Like me."

"You can call it whatever you want. But it might make life around here a little better for you and might give you a chance to show us what you really know."

"I don't know anything."

"That's not true." I just look down at my lap. It isn't very interesting, but I don't know what else to do. I can't think straight around this teacher lady. She twists me up a bit, trying to make me think I can do things I know I can't do. I have enough problems with the whole fostergirl garbage without adding sped to my list of names.

But at the same time, it would be kind of OK to find a way to make school less gross if I have to stick it out for two more years.

Like I say, twisted up.

"I just don't know. I don't need any more hassles." Rhiannon's half-smile face pops into my brain without being invited.

"If you're having problems, Sadie, you can talk to me. About anything."

"I don't need talking." I've already done too much of that.

"All right. I'll leave you to think about this a bit. I wrote down my resource schedule so you'll know when I'm in there. If you decide you want to come down and see me, you can just come if it's during lunch. If it's during class, come here for a pass first."

Yeah, like I'm going to advertise!

"OK." I get up to leave. She looks kind of disappointed, like she actually cares whether I look at her talking computer game or not. She's kind of a weird teacher. She must not have any life at all if she can spend this much time worrying about one hopeless case.

Lunch is pretty much over by the time I get back into the hall. I head toward my next class, figuring to shock the teacher by being early for once.

"Sadie! I've been looking everywhere for you! It's too bad you couldn't come over on the weekend. It was pretty boring for me 'cause I had to hang out with Chandra, who is not interested in anything I like at all. I guess you aren't either, but that doesn't matter because at least we're the same age and everything. I know you don't like the group home but it must be kind of nice to have a couple of girls around the same age, although I could see on Saturday that there is some stress there, which isn't surprising. That kind of stuff has happened few times around our place too." She stops for breath, looking at me. She seems to be on hyper drive, her words flying out of her mouth at top speed. She still has that weird almost smile that makes me feel uncomfortable. I look at her, trying to think of what to say. This time Alisha's ugly face pops into my head, along with her ugly words. I know she isn't any big authority on life in general, but the things she said make sense to me. Rhiannon is weird for sure, but she isn't fostergirl weird. She has two parents and one house that she's been in forever. She's a nerd and a "good" girl. I bet she's never been within ten feet of a cigarette or booze or anything else. We have nothing in common, except that she collects foster kids and I am one.

"I'm going to be late for class. I have English this period today, and I don't want to deal with Wilson's crap." I turn away without looking directly at her and walk down the hall. I think for a second of turning around to see her reaction, but I don't do it. She won't care anyway. She's probably off looking for Buffy to see if she wants to be friends instead of me.

At least that's what I tell myself.

chapter 12

"I'm going home this weekend!" Alisha's voice slams into me as I walk into my room. It's the last thing in the world I want to listen to right now. My head is aching and my throat hurts. Hopefully I have some deadly disease that will keep me out of school and spread to Alisha so that her throat swells up permanently and she can't talk at me anymore.

"Did you hear me? I'm going home. My social twit just called and told me mom is doing good this week, and they approved a visit. Supervised, which sucks large, but they're letting my nana do it."

"Your *nana*?" The word "nana" is dumb enough, but coming out of Alisha's mouth it sounds like some sort of weird fruit.

"My grandmother. She's my mom's mom."

"Oh. Yeah. Whatever." Grandmother. I forgot about those. Wonder if I have one?

"Yeah. She's pretty cool, but not as cool as my mom. She

doesn't do anything that gets the cops excited, at least not where anyone can see her."

"Why don't you live with her?" Why do I ask questions I don't want to know the answer to?

"Oh, she's too old to want someone my age around all of the time. She needs her peace and quiet after looking after my mom. Mom was kind of wild." She smiles like she's all proud.

"Oh."

"Anyway, she doesn't mind coming for the weekend 'cause Mom is in charge of me, and she's kind of in charge of mom, and the social twit said that's OK 'cause Nana doesn't have any charges against her, so it's all good. We're going to watch R-rated movies and eat chocolate ice cream right until we puke."

"Sounds like fun." I hate ice cream. It's too cold.

"It will be amazing. Better than being in this hole in the wall." She kicks the wall hard. A thump comes back through the wall.

"Buffy." We both say it at the same time and kind of laugh.

"Better be careful or she'll lose it again and run in here trying to slay us." Alisha thinks it's funny to use the same joke a million times. I don't.

"What's up with her, anyway? Never seen anyone go so fast from zero to sixty before. It's like she's only got two speeds. Relatively OK and totally out of control."

"She's nuts on account of her father. He did some pretty gross stuff to her and no one believed her at first. At least that's what she told me one time. I don't know why she told me anything, because she hates me and all, but she was crying and stuff, and I guess it just came out, you know? She told me her dad liked to make movies about sicko adults doing things to little kids that he sold to other sickos. When she was really little he just made her watch, but when she got to be old enough, he made her the star of the kiddy porn creep show."

"Old enough?"

"Yeah, like eight or nine, I think she said. Anyway, she told her aunt about it, and her aunt didn't believe her and called her dad and told him that Buffy was lying about him. He went ballistic and waled on her. She kept it a secret after that for a real long time. She said she had to, or he would have killed her. I don't know if that part's true or not. Anyway, some teacher at school noticed something was off with her and somehow got her to spill. You know how teachers like to get in your face and make trouble."

"Her dad in jail?"

"Don't think so. By the time the cops raided the house there wasn't anything there. But I guess they believed enough so that Buffy went into the system."

"Sucks."

"Totally. I'd feel sorry for her, but she's such a pain in the ass that I keep forgetting to." Alisha laughs at herself and rolls over onto her back. She actually stops talking for thirty seconds, probably dreaming of her exciting weekend with Nana and Mommy.

The silence is nice, and after a while I drift off into dreamland where I hope I don't dream.

I don't know how long I was out, but it's still dark when I hear a voice at the door.

"Alisha, I need to talk to you." It's Sandi, which is surprising, because it isn't even her shift. I open my eyes and watch Alisha sit up.

"Sandi, it's the middle of the night! I need my sleep. I'm going home. I need to rest up so I can stay up all night."

"Alisha, come on downstairs. Marianne is here."

"What's my social witch doing here? She run out of people to torture?" Alisha tries to sound tough, but she sounds scared instead.

"Just come with me. Let Sadie sleep." I close my eyes quick. I don't want to be involved in whatever drama is coming.

It comes a few minutes later, and everyone in the neighborhood probably got involved when they heard the screaming. At first it sounds like someone is beating on Alisha, and I actually jump out of bed and start running downstairs to save her. I stop halfway down when I see that she isn't being smacked with a bat.

"Shut up! You're lying to me!" Alisha is screaming at her social worker and putting her hands over Marianne's mouth, like she's trying to push her words back into her.

"I'm so sorry, honey. I know this is hard."

"Shut up, I said! I'm not your honey and you don't know anything!" She jumps at her, looking like she's going to claw her face off. Sandi steps in and takes her by the wrists, really gently, and looks at her right in the eyes.

"Alisha. I need you to sit down. I know I can't possibly understand how you feel, but you need to sit down. Just sit down. Come on now, just sit down." She says it over and over, while she quietly and slowly moves Alisha down onto the couch. She crouches down in front of her, still holding her wrists. Alisha sits down and her head drops down on her chest like she's knocked out. All of a sudden she starts to cry, this horrible loud crying. Sandi just reaches up and grabs her in a bear hug, while Alisha cries and cries and cries. She's saying the same word over and over. At first I can't make it out, but then I realize what she's saying.

Mommy.

I stay listening on the stairs for a while until I hear the whole story. I guess Alisha's mom accidentally walked in front of a truck and was killed instantly. I can hear Alisha kind of moaning, and she asks them did it hurt. They tell her no, that it was fast and that she didn't know what happened. They keep on telling her it was an accident. They tell her that so many times that I start to wonder if it's really true.

I sneak back up the stairs. Buffy is standing in the hall.

"Her mom?" She looks kind of teary eyed.

"Yeah."

"Sucks." She turns away and goes back into her room.

I go into our room. Buffy's right. This totally sucks. Sitting on my bed, I hug my knees to my chest and rock back and forth a little, wondering what's going to happen now.

I'm hoping Alisha doesn't come back up here because I don't know what to say. I don't know how to deal with someone who's totally freaked because her mom's dead.

She was so excited about going to her mom's house to watch stupid movies. All she talks about every night is how great her mom is and how she can't wait to go home and how wonderful it all will be.

Now her mom's dead, and Alisha's got no one but her nana who's too old to look after her.

How does it feel to lose your mom? Obviously pretty bad because Alisha looked like the whole world had crashed onto her head. Did I feel that way when I was little and my mom disappeared? I don't remember losing her. I don't even remember having her.

Alisha believed her mom loved her and wanted her, even though it always looked to me that her mom liked drinking booze better than being a mom. It was like it didn't matter what her mom did, Alisha still wanted her. I knew some other kids like that, fosterkids who talked about how wonderful their parents were even though they had kicked them around or forgotten to feed them. Weird. What is it that makes kids love parents who don't deserve to be loved?

I know one thing. I'll never waste one single emotion on my mother.

I close my eyes and sit and rock and listen to the soft sounds coming from downstairs. My eyes sting and my throat still hurts.

I really must be getting the flu.

chapter 13

Alisha's grandmother lives in a city about a forty-minute drive from MacAvoy. Alisha went there the morning after finding out about her mom so she could be with her family for the funeral. I didn't talk to her before she left, which was good, because there isn't anything I could say to her that would make any difference. What can you say to someone whose mom just walked in front of a truck?

"Sadie, will you be coming with us?" Sandi asks me at supper that night. I hadn't been paying attention to whatever they had all been babbling about. I eat when it's eating time. I don't get why people think eating time is a good time to be talking. I don't want to see the mushed-up mess inside their mouths. Ruins my appetite.

"Sadie?" Obviously I'm still not listening.

"Sorry, I was eating. Where?" Not that I want to know.

"I was asking you if you will be coming with us to the funeral. It's on Thursday afternoon. You'd have to miss classes."

"I don't know." Missing classes isn't really the point here. I don't do funerals. I've never been to a funeral in my life. I don't think I want to go to some church and watch a bunch of strangers cry and moan about Alisha's mother, who I never even met. What are funerals for, anyway? The ones I've seen on TV only seem to make everyone feel like garbage.

"It's up to you. Krista and Kendra will be staying here with Sarah, so there isn't any problem if you want to stay here. Buffy is going to come with me."

"To the funeral. Really." I look at Buffy.

"Alisha doesn't have much family. She'll need our support." She's kidding, right? All I have ever seen Alisha and Buffy do was to try to kill each other, or at the very least drive each other crazy. Why would Buffy think Alisha would want to see her at something as awful as a funeral?

"We're not her family."

"No, but we are the people she lives with. You're her roommate. You should want to come." She's talking in this calm, almost normal voice like she's saying normal things. Buffy standing up for Alisha is not normal.

"I haven't been her roommate very long." I'm not sure what that has to do with anything, but it seems like a good comeback.

"It doesn't matter. You can come if you feel comfortable. Otherwise you can stay here with the others." Sandi gives Buffy a look that is supposed to shut her up.

"Why aren't the Ks going? They've known her longer than me." They'd left the table by now and it was just the three of us. Buffy looks at me like I'm the dumbest jerk on earth.

"Are you kidding? After what Krista went through? She doesn't go anywhere near anything to do with death or dying."

"What are you talking about?"

"Buffy. Private information." Sandi looks at her, shakes her head. I look at both of them. How nice for them. They have little secrets.

"Fine, but I think it's stupid. We have a right to know who we live with." The calm voice is gone. Buffy walks out of the room without another word about how supportive we need to be. I think she must have forgotten that we were talking about Alisha.

"I'm sorry, Sadie. I know it seems like keeping secrets, but you know the personal privacy rule. If Krista wants to share, that's up to her."

"I'd be just as happy if she didn't. I don't need any more sad little stories. There's enough drama around here as it is."

"Anyway, if you need time to decide about Alisha, take it. I don't need to know until tomorrow." Sandi walks out of the room, leaving me alone with the dishes.

I don't need time. I don't want to go to some funeral where Buffy is going to fake caring about Alisha, and Alisha is going to fake caring that Buffy cares. Or something like that. I don't want to meet Alisha's nana, or whatever she calls her, and I don't want to stand around watching strangers cry. Alisha's not my sister. She's not even my friend. She's my roommate. That's it.

It's my night to wash up, so I take my time over the dishes and table cloths. I usually do it as fast as I can, but tonight it seems better than the possibility that I might have to talk to someone. This works for about twenty minutes, and then Buffy walks back into the kitchen.

"I don't care about Sandi's rules. They don't make sense. If you have to live with people, you have to know who they are. I know Alisha told you a bunch of stuff about me."

"Not really."

"You don't have to lie. I know her mouth never stops moving. It's OK. I have nothing to hide." She looks at me like she thinks I might care.

"She didn't say much. I don't remember, anyway." I hope she's not expecting to hear anything interesting about my life. I'm not one to share.

"Whatever. Anyway, Krista had an incident a couple of years before she ended up here."

"An incident." Should keep my mouth shut. Anything I say will just encourage her.

"That's what they called it. I don't know what I would call it. Something worse than 'incident.' Anyway, when she was seven or eight or whatever, she came home from school one day and found her house empty. Her dad was supposed to be there because her mom had walked out on them a few months before. She didn't freak out at first 'cause she figured he was at the store or whatever, so she went to the kitchen to get a snack. He was hanging from the ceiling fan. Rumor is he used her Hello Kitty skipping rope to do it."

"That sucks." I can't think of anything else to say. So many things just plain suck in this world.

"Gets worse. She calls nine-one-one and they don't realize she's just a kid at first. They tell her to hold his legs. The cops get there and she's holding his legs, rocking him and singing to him to keep him awake. The poor kid didn't even know he was dead. Or didn't want to. Anyway, her mom didn't want to come back and get her so she ended up in foster care, and then here. She's so quiet, you'd be shocked if you saw how freaked out she gets if anyone mentions death or dying or anything. We have to be careful what we watch on the boob tube, too."

"I never noticed." I don't notice much. I never even wondered about Krista. To be honest, I'm not sure which one of the Ks she is.

"What about Kendra?" What am I doing? I don't want to know any more about this stuff. I mean, I know that kids don't end up in places like MacAvoy because they have happy little lives with perfect little parents, but I don't need to know the details of everyone's misery. I have to learn to keep my mouth shut. A few weeks hanging around Rhiannon and my tongue seems to be out of control. Good thing she's gone.

"Kendra doesn't have death issues. She's just always with Krista so she'll stick back here. It's hard to believe they didn't even know each other before they came here. They just totally lean on each other. It's kind of weird. Kendra misses her sister, I think. She's in a foster home back in the town they came from. Their mom's in jail. Drugs, I think. Their dad's trying to clean up his act so he can get them back, but so far no luck."

"How do you know all of this?"

"I ask."

"Oh." Never thought of that. The dishes are pretty sparkling clean. They haven't done the job of helping me avoid people, so I just put them away and turn to go. Buffy touches my arm for a tiny piece of a second, too small for me to react.

"I know you all think I'm nuts and I probably am. I also know you think I'm a total pain. I can live with that. We don't have to like each other, but there aren't too many people out there who give a crap about any of us.... I still think we need to look out for each other a bit."

"Not sure what that would look like."

"Might have to look like going to a funeral." She walks out of the room, leaving me to think about things I don't want to think about.

chapter 14

"What am I supposed to wear?" I can't believe that I'm doing this. Getting dressed to go to the funeral of someone I never met because someone I don't like told me I should. I'm not even sure why I'm going. I don't particularly like Alisha, either.

"Just something clean and not skanky." Buffy giving me fashion advice.

"Have you ever seen me wear something skanky?" I dress in what's comfortable. Jeans, T-shirt, sweater. I don't think about it much. I like to keep covered up. My body's no one's business but mine.

"No. Guess I was thinking about Alisha."

"Nice. Especially today." My voice is all muffled by the sweatshirt I'm pulling over my head. I sniff it as it comes down past my nose. Smells clean.

"I wasn't being mean. Alisha likes to look sexy, is all. She likes to show off her boobs. Wish I had a pair like her." She looks down at her chest, which I have to agree isn't too impressive. I don't look at mine, because I don't care about the size of my body parts, especially those ones. In my experience, other people are way too interested in them, so it's best to keep them out of sight.

"Well, I doubt she'll be feeling too sexy today."

"Yeah. It must be so awful to know your mom is dead. I mean, I don't really ever see mine or anything, but at least I know she's alive. Somewhere." Buffy looks at me, kind of sad eyed.

"Sure. Whatever." I kind of shrug.

"What about you?"

"What about me what?" I know what she wants me to say.

"You never talk about your mom or dad or whatever."

"No, I don't."

"It helps sometimes, you know. Just to talk about things and get them off your chest."

"I don't need to talk about anything." Please go away now!

"Whatever. Sandi's probably waiting for us downstairs. You better hurry up." She kind of stomps out of the room, like she's mad at me for not spilling my guts to her. Why do people always say that talking about things makes you feel better? It doesn't. Things should be kept safely locked up inside of you. Talking about them lets them loose and then you can't always catch them and put them away again.

I run my fingers through my hair and pull my sweatshirt down over the waistband of my jeans. I put my running shoes on and head downstairs to face whatever I'm facing today.

Buffy's right for once, and Sandi is ready and waiting. She looks different to me, all dressed up like a real adult. She has on a skirt and jacket and shoes with heels. A big change from her usual jeans and T-shirt. A skirt and heels wouldn't be such a good idea around here, when you never know when you might have to have a spontaneous wrestling match with a whacked-out grouphomegirl. She stands up, taller than usual, and looks down at me. She opens her mouth as if to make a comment on my clothes, but she swallows it. Good thing, because if she says one word, I'm out of here.

The ride to the church is a quiet one. No one can think of anything to say, I guess. Not that Buffy and I ever have anything particularly interesting to say to one another. She's such a weird kid. I guess her—what did Alisha call it?—*kiddy porn freak show* might account for it. I guess I know what it feels like to have everyone think you're a liar. I had a couple of pseudomoms who blamed me for everything that happened in the house, even though most of it was caused by their own biokids. Biokids are treated like they can do no wrong. Maybe pseudoparents take in fostergirls so that they can have someone to blame for their biokids' screw ups.

We get to the church too fast for my liking. I'm really wishing that I could just wait in the car. I still can't believe I'm here. Anything would be better than this, even sitting at home watching G-rated movies with the Ks and Sarah. Sandi pulls into the parking lot, which is mostly empty. Guess Alisha's mom wasn't too popular around here.

The church is ridiculously big. Endless pews fill it up from front to back. The windows make the sunlight come in all different colors through the stained glass. Everyone seems to have splotches of color on them, like they're the losers in a paintball war. The ceiling is so high you have to practically do a back walkover to see it. There are pipes going up the back of the church from floor to ceiling, ready to fill the place with the deadly church music that makes you want to tear your ears off and sit on them.

I know that I used to go to church. Mrs. Sampson definitely made me go, but I think a couple of other pseudomoms did, too, when I was small. Not sure exactly when or where, but I have blurred memories of using the time in the pews to catch up on my sleep and being elbowed and poked quite a bit by other kids either trying to wake me up or trying to get me in trouble. Probably both.

There are only a few pews filled with people near the front of the church. I really, really want to sit at the very back where I can be invisible, but Sandi leads us right up to the next available seat, about five rows back from the front. Close enough to see all of the action. Great.

Alisha isn't anywhere to be seen. That's even more great. I'm here and she decides to skip the whole deal. That would be exactly what she would do. So selfish. I open my mouth to say something about it to Sandi, but just then the obnoxious church music starts. It's crazy loud, coming from all those pipes and rising up to the ceiling. There aren't enough people here to absorb the sound, and it pounds us down into the seats. I wonder how much it will hurt when I have to rip my ears off.

Everyone stands up, struggling out from under the music. I stand up, too, even though I don't know why. It's as if someone's holding up a cue card telling us what to do. Sandi turns her head toward the back of the church. Now I see what's going on. I might have to take my eyes out, too. I think it's time to go home. Really.

The coffin is slowly slithering up the aisle, a couple of men on each side moving it along. The men look all serious and sort of angry to me. I wonder if they're friends of Alisha's mom or just guys paid to look annoyed at funerals. Behind the coffin comes the family. Alisha and a lady I guess is her nana lead the way. Alisha is not dressed skanky. She has a black sweater on and black pants.

Her hair is pulled back into some kind of bun deal. She usually has it brushed out as full as she can, all wild and frizzy with red and blue streaks mixed into the black fuzz. She looks like an alternate version of herself today, a version from some universe where she's some kind of normal person. Her nana doesn't look anything like her. She's a tiny little woman who looks like she might fall over if you blow on her too hard. No wonder she thought Alisha might be too much to look after. Alisha could eat her for breakfast and still be hungry for lunch.

Alisha isn't crying or anything. She has the same look on her face as the coffin men. Maybe the funeral director teaches them that before they come in. She doesn't look at us when she passes by. Her eyes are glued to the coffin where her mom is. Mine aren't. I'm still thinking about taking them out and putting them in my pocket, along with my ears. I don't want to look at the coffin and wonder what the woman inside looks like. Why do they do this, anyway? It seems kind of disrespectful to me. I mean, we know she's dead already. We don't need the whole box-in-the-room deal to make it more obvious to us. It seems like it just makes it more painful for the people who are having a rough time already. I never met this woman, and I don't really even know Alisha, and I still feel like I want to look at anything except the front of the room where death is lying.

The service itself is long and drawn out. Lots of prayers and standing up and sitting down. The priest gives a speech about Alisha's mother that makes her sound like some kind of angel instead of an alcoholic who couldn't take care of her own kid. A few people are kind of sniffling by now. Buffy is crying into her Kleenex, and Sandi has her arm around her.

It finally ends, and the whole bizarre funeral parade moves

back the other way. Alisha's nana is crying now. Alisha walks beside her. She isn't crying yet. She's just kind of hugging herself and looking mad. She looks over at me as she walks by this time. She stops looking mad for a second and looks kind of surprised. I don't know what to do, so I do a stupid little wave thing. She waves back and actually kind of smiles. Just for a second. Then her eyes go black again and she stares straight ahead as she joins the parade, a sad clown dressed in someone else's clothes.

I breathe a sigh of relief. It's over, and now we can go home.

"We'll just stay at the reception for a few minutes and then go," Sandi says to us. The reception? What the hell is that?

"The what?" I ask, even though I'm pretty sure I don't want to know. Buffy looks at me like I'm an idiot, which is the way she usually looks at me. At least it's something familiar.

"The reception. They have food and drinks so we can mingle and talk."

"Mingle and talk? About what?" I thought they were taking the parade to the graveyard to put Alisha's mom in the ground so she could have some peace and quiet.

"People like to share memories of the person who died or to share their condolences with the family," Sandi says.

"I didn't know Alisha's mom and I don't know her family."

"But you know Alisha." Sandi heads off toward the back of the church and leads the way to the reception. I didn't know they served food and drinks at funerals; it's like some kind of bizarre party. I don't think I like the idea that people might have a good time at my funeral. Not that there will be any people at my funeral. Who would come? Why do I care? Why am I thinking about this? Maybe they have real drinks, and I can sneak a couple and forget this whole day while I'm still living it.

We're just walking into the party room when I feel a tap on my arm.

"Sadie?"

I kind of spin around, surprised that anyone here knows my name.

"What are you doing here?" I ask Rhiannon, who is standing there with her mom. I hadn't noticed them in the church.

"We've known Alisha for a while. We felt we should pay our respects." Her mom's voice is quiet but there's something in it that makes me wonder if Rhiannon told her that we don't hang out any more.

"Alisha lived with us when she was younger for a while. Her mom ended up getting her back and then things fell apart, but by the time she needed a home again, we were all full. She's always been kind of upset about that." Rhiannon's voice is quiet like her mom's. There's something in it, too. I'm not so good at reading voices so I don't know what it is. I just know something's there and it isn't great.

"I didn't know that." Kind of stating the obvious, but it's all I can think of in the moment. I've been living with Alisha and hanging out with Rhiannon and neither of them say anything about knowing each other, even after the whole video store drama? More secrets.

"I guess it never came up."

"Guess not." Secrets don't usually come up unless you want them to. We stand there in the doorway. Rhiannon's mom has already moved into the room, along with Sandi and Buffy. All three of them are standing with Alisha and her nana. Rhiannon's mom gives Alisha a big hug and kind of rubs her back, talking to her for a few moments. I stand there staring, feeling like an audience member watching a movie where I don't really know the actors, and I'm wondering what's going to happen next. Maybe they have popcorn. Rhiannon's watching, too. I don't say anything to her, because I don't know what to say.

"I guess I'll go talk to Alisha," she says, not really looking at me. I watch as she joins the others. She comes up to where her mom is still holding Alisha, who seems to be crying by now. Wonder what Ms. Kerry said to her to make her cry? Rhiannon puts her arm around Alisha also, which is amazing on so many levels. Alisha trashed her last time she saw her and now Rhiannon's acting like she's her best friend. I guess that's what it is though, acting. Everyone performing their role because they're at a funeral and they have to do a good job for all the other actors. And the Oscar for Biggest Hypocrite goes to…

Me.

I can't do this any more. Enough. I don't want to be here. I don't want to eat or drink or hug or condole. I just want to go away.

I head out to the car. It's locked, of course, so I just lean against the hood, waiting for the movie to end so we can go.

chapter 15

If my life really was a movie, the audience would have left by now, due to total boredom. All I do these days is go to school, come back to MacAvoy and pretend to work on school stuff, go to bed, and then get up and start the whole exciting cycle over again. School is full of nerd babies and people who think they're cool but aren't. I got so bored one day I even wandered back to see if the dumpster people were still there to soak in a little smoke and conversation. They're still there, and I got plenty of smoke but not much conversation. Still boring.

Lunchtime is the worst. There's no one I want to talk to, and nowhere I actually want to go. The cafeteria is full of empty noise. The library is full of empty silence. My head is just plain empty.

It's all even crappier today because it's raining. So, I'm just wandering around the halls, feeling sorry for myself, wishing the rain would stop, and trying to find something to make the time pass by. I have this weird memory flash of being a little kid and thinking that rain meant the angels were crying. It made me feel sad. Don't know where I would have gotten that idea. Maybe it was during my Sunday school days.

I wonder what Rhiannon does on rainy days. Probably hangs out in the science lab with the other geeks. Not that I care. She doesn't care, either. She barely talks to me in science class now and doesn't try to find me anywhere else. Not that I care.

I end up on the second floor. Right outside the resource room. I don't think I walked here on purpose. I don't want to be a part of the whole sped scene. I look in the window of the door at the speds sitting at their sped desks. Jackson is there, walking around and talking to people. There are about six kids in there, all different ages it looks like. Don't recognize anyone, but that doesn't surprise me. Haven't exactly joined too many social clubs here.

"Hi Sadie, are you coming in?" Jackson's somehow managed to get to the door and get it open without me even seeing her. Too preoccupied with staring at the kids. Stupid Sadie.

"What?" I heard her, but I don't have an answer so I play dumb. Unfortunately, I'm not really acting.

"I said, are you coming in?" I can still hear her. Of course she's talking louder this time because she thinks I didn't hear her, which is just wonderful because now everyone in the classroom, and probably all the way down to the cafeteria, can hear her inviting me into her little house of horror.

"I guess so." The words come out of my mouth without getting my brain involved in the decision making. This is becoming a really annoying habit. My legs join the mutiny, and I find myself walking into the room to join the reject squad.

No one seems remotely interested in me when I come in, which is just fine, because I'm not interested in any of them, either.

Although I kind of wonder why they all look relatively happy to be there. I mean no one's dancing on top of their desk or anything, but no one looks like they want to jump out the window, either. *I* want to jump out the window, but instead I'm following Jackson over to a row of lonely-looking computers, with the exception of a couple that have kids sitting at them. One of the kids is typing like a normal person. The other is wearing headphones and staring at some kind of weird-looking deal where words are flashing in different colors on the screen.

"I'm glad you decided to come and see me. I've been wondering when you might drop by. I guess it's been a rough few days with Alisha having such a tough time."

"Rough for Alisha." Alisha had only stayed with her nana for a day before coming back to MacAvoy. I was totally nervous when she first came back. I didn't know what to say to her and was afraid she'd want to talk about her feelings or something. Alisha never had trouble spouting off about anything that was bugging her, and this was a pretty big anything. I figured I'd be up half the night listening to her going on about how terrible her life is 'cause her mom died.

The weird thing is, so far she's just been really quiet. I mean, really quiet. She doesn't say anything at all, except "pass the butter" or whatever. It's spooky. It's like she went away for a couple of days and came back with someone else's personality. A really quiet person's. Not that I'm complaining, because I didn't really like the loud version, but I had gotten kind of used to her. This is like having a new roommate all over again.

"Why don't you come down to the end so we can talk without disturbing anyone else."

Jackson walks down to the very last computer in the row and

sits down, patting the chair beside her. I sit down, still wondering what I'm doing here. She hands me some headphones. Not the big dorky-looking ones the other kid has on, but a pair of those little ear-bud things that look like they should be attached to an MP3 player. I sit with them in my hand and look at her.

"This is the program I was telling you about in my office. We have it on all the computers in the school. I'll show you how it works, and then you can try it with the earphones on."

"Whatever." I'll just stay for a few minutes and listen to her. Unbelievably, there isn't anything better to do with my time.

So she starts explaining. Basically, it's this program that makes the computer read stuff to you. Anything that's already on a computer or CD and anything you can scan into it. The words can come at you at all different speeds, and there are different voices you can choose from that all sound like robots from some kind of sci-fi movie. You can make it read one word at a time or whole sentences. The words that are coming at you are lit up or highlighted or whatever you call it. You can stop on a word and get the definition if you don't know what it means.

"So, basically this thing lets you totally cheat." Cool.

"A lot of people see it that way. I'm not sure who you're cheating, though. I mean, you're past the age where we're checking to see if you can read the words or not, right? Your teachers aren't trying to figure out if you know the sounds the alphabet makes. They want to know if you understand what you are reading about."

"But I'm not reading. The computer is."

"But the computer isn't telling you what it all means. It might define a word or two but it doesn't put it all together for you. Understanding the ideas has to come from you."

"So, you're telling me it's OK to sit here and let the computer do the reading for me?" Not that I've ever had a problem with cheating as a way to survive school, but this seems like something that would be pretty hard to hide.

"The computer is deciphering the letters and telling you what the words are. The reading part comes from you listening and interpreting and understanding."

"I still don't really get what you're saying."

"That's OK. There are a lot of adults who don't get it, either. The bottom line is that this is not cheating. I wear glasses, right?"

"Yeah."

"If I take them off, I can't see the letters on the screen any more, so I can't read. Is it cheating for me to put my glasses on so I can read the letters?"

"No, but that's different."

"How?"

"You need your glasses to see. It's like, physical or whatever."

"There you go. It's the same for lots of kids who have trouble reading. There can be physical reasons that the letters they see don't make sense to them. I don't know for sure that's what happens with you, but it's possible. One way to help find out is to try reading a different way. The computer is kind of like your glasses."

"I don't need people getting on my case about being stupid."

"It's like I told you before—we can work on this here. Everyone who works in here has their own version of needing 'glasses.' If this works out for you, it will be your decision if you get to the point where you feel you can work with it in other classrooms or the library."

"Don't think that will happen." Although I kind of wonder what it would be like to actually be able to listen to the twenty pages the science teacher always tells us to read when she's sick of teaching us in class. Then I wonder how many people would laugh at me sitting at the computer with my little yellow words flashing at me because I'm too brain dead to read them the old-fashioned way.

"Will you at least come here and work on some of your assignments just to see if it makes a difference?"

"Maybe. There's not much to do around here at lunchtime, anyway."

"Good. I have a writing program I'd like to show you as well, but we'll save that for another day." She makes it sound like we're going to be doing something interesting, like skipping class and heading for an R-rated movie or something.

"Can't wait." I pull the ear buds out and hand them back to her.

"You hold on to them. They're yours for when you need to use them." She smiles and heads back over to talk to another kid. No one is paying any attention to me. I look at the little plastic earphones in my hand and wonder about all the things Jackson is telling me. How could my sucking at reading be physical? I can see and I can hear. I just can't make sense of the stupid words when too many of them gang up on me.

The bell is ringing in my ears now, which today means science class, which means Rhiannon. Now that she's a lot quieter in class than she used to be, I should be able to hear the teacher a little more. Guess that's a good thing if I want to pass. Bad if I want to stay awake. I have to admit, Rhiannon's version of things was always a little more interesting than the teacher's. She still keeps her book angled so that I can see the answers to the endless questions the teacher makes us answer, but I don't feel right copying from her any more. It's probably just more of her whole "pity the poor fostergirl" routine, anyway.

I get to class, and everyone is looking happy for a change, which can only mean one thing. A supply teacher. Which means an independent work period, which means the lady at the front of the room gets paid to tell us to read thirty pages of boring science notes and to answer a gazillion questions. For just a second I wonder if I should take my book down to the resource room and try out the computer thing. Just for a second. Then I look around the class at everyone laughing and talking and reading. I'm already in the room and would have to ask permission to leave. I'm not doing that in front of everyone. Not that I care about any of their pathetic opinions, but it's still no one's business.

So I sit and stare at the words. It's not worth the effort to read them, so I just listen to the laughing and the talking. Rhiannon reads for a while, and then gives up and looks at me. Her eyes look different than they used to somehow. I mean, they're the same color and everything, but it's almost like they're a different shade. Duller somehow. Which is stupid. Obviously I just forgot what they look like.

"How's Alisha?"

"Not great."

"It must be so hard for her. How are you?"

"Me? I'm fine."

"I was just wondering. I mean, it's probably hard for you, too. It's hard being around someone who's sad like that. One of our kids lost his mom a few years back. It was really tough."

"One of *your* kids." Like it was something she owned, like a cat or a dog.

"Yes. I mean, I guess they aren't my kids, but you know what I mean."

"Actually I don't. I don't collect foster kids."

"What are you talking about?"

"You know what I'm talking about." I don't know why I feel angry with her. I don't care what she does or thinks.

"I'm not sure. You mean that stuff Alisha said that night? That's what's been going on all this time? Is that why you don't want to be my friend?" Her eyes spark a little and I swear they change color again. I must be going nuts.

"I don't need friends. I'm pretty sure I told you that before."

"Well, I thought we were friends. Or at least working on it. And all of a sudden you just decide I'm some kind of freak or something and stop talking to me. All because of something Alisha said because my mom is a foster mom?" Now she closes her eyes and shakes her head. Who's she to shake her head at me? She's the one at fault here.

"Yeah, well if we're such good friends, why didn't you tell me you know Alisha? Not that I'm any expert, but I'm pretty sure friends are supposed to be honest with each other." I look directly at her, waiting. Like to see her talk her way out of this one! She opens her eyes and looks at me. Her head is still kind of shaking, and she rolls her eyes a little. First a head shake and then an eye roll? If it was anyone else, I'd be smacking her so hard that her head would be shaking and her eyes rolling for a week. Besides, we're sitting in class, and I'm pretty sure that would be considered an act of violence. Rhiannon doesn't say anything right away. Actually, she's quiet for so long that I start to think that the conversation is over. Fine with me. I don't want to talk to her anyway.

"That was the wrong thing to do. I should have said something. It's just that she was really upset when she couldn't come back to us and she decided to hate us and I didn't want her saying things about me to you and scaring you off. I thought if I didn't tell you, it wouldn't come up. I guess that was stupid because it kind of came up and messed up anyway."

"Doesn't make the things she said any less true." Except that Alisha kept the secret away from me, too. I can't trust either of them. So, who do I believe?

It made sense when I was thinking about it back at MacAvoy. Now it's getting all turned upside down and backwards, and I can't find the thoughts any more.

"So, basically you've decided that you don't like me because my mom takes in foster kids. Well, join the crowd." She shakes her head again, but this time I don't feel like hitting her. She looks kind of sad or something. It's no fun hitting sad people.

"What do you mean?"

"This is a really small town, Sadie, and people around here have their own ideas of what normal is. I'm not it. My family isn't it. Lots of kids think we're weird because we have all these kids from all over. We even had a couple of neighbors start a petition once to ask us to move or stop taking in kids who had problems."

"They wanted you to stop collecting foster kids?"

"We don't *collect* foster kids. My parents try to help kids who don't have homes." Her volume rises and a couple of kids stop throwing paper airplanes long enough to look our way. I stare them down, and they go back to trying to hit the teacher in the back.

"Like me." Poor little fostergirl.

"Maybe. But you being in foster care had nothing to do with me trying to be friends. I don't exactly have a lot of people lining up to hang out with me. I didn't even know who you were that first day I saw you. You were just someone new and I thought I'd try to get to know you. We seemed to get along OK. That's it!"

She smacks her hand down like she's ending the sentence with an exclamation point.

"That's it? Really." I'm trying to hold onto Alisha's words but they're slipping under Rhiannon's.

"Actually no, that's not it. There is one more thing. There's this name some kids used to call me when they were trying to make me feel like crap. Actually there are lots of them, but this one might interest you."

"Yeah, why is that?"

"They used to call me fostergirl."

She shakes her head one last time and goes back to reading her science book. I can't think of anything to say that would make any sense, so I go back to pretending to read my science book and trying not to think about other people's words.

chapter 16

"Fostergirl. Fostergirl." The voice is whispering, but it's loud enough to penetrate my brain. I can't see who it is. It's too dark. My stupid nightlight is still burnt out, and I can't seem to reach up and find the light switch. The voice keeps following me as I run down the hall. My feet are bare, so they don't make any noise, but my breathing is so loud I think the whole world can hear me coming. I don't know what I'm afraid of. I don't know who the voice belongs to or if they want to hurt me, but I run anyway. I don't know where to run to, though. I can't figure out where to hide and there doesn't seem to be anyone home to protect me, so I just run.

"You can run, little fostergirl, but you can't hide." The voice definitely sounds threatening now. I run down the stairs and into the kitchen, hoping someone will be there who will grab me and hide me from the whisper. But the kitchen is empty, and I run into the wall, wishing it was a door. I crouch down in the corner. Maybe if I'm small enough the voice won't get me and do whatever it's going to do. I'm shaking, and I can feel stupid baby tears starting down my cheeks. I want someone to come and pick me up and take me somewhere safe.

"Leave me alone!" I'm shouting, but the sound comes out a tear-filled whisper.

"Sadie?" A different voice breaks in and jolts me awake. Alisha. I'm in bed having one of my idiot nightmares. And Alisha, whose real life is a nightmare, is sitting there looking at me like I'm nuts. Could this get any better?

"Sorry. Guess I'm like talking in my sleep or something lame like that." I roll away against the wall and stare at a spot where the paint has worn away. The room used to be pink but now it's brown. Good thing. Don't think I could stand living in a pink room.

"You sounded upset. Like scared or something."

"I wasn't scared. Just stupid. Sorry I woke you." Go to sleep, Alisha.

"I wasn't sleeping. I don't sleep much these days."

"Oh." I hope she isn't suddenly in the mood for a chat, because I just want to find a dreamless sleep for the rest of the night.

"Sadie, can I talk to you?"

"OK." Yeah, go ahead and talk, but do I have to listen? I roll back so I can look at her. She's sitting up in bed, her knees pulled up to her chest like she's trying to hug herself. Her head is on her knees and her eyes are closed. For a second I think my luck has changed and she's fallen asleep.

"I think my mom killed herself." She still has her head down which is good, because I don't know what to do with that sentence. I'm pretty sure she's right about that, but I don't want her to see that in my eyes.

"Why?" Probably a stupid question.

"Why do I think it wasn't really an accident, or why do I think she would want to kill herself?" She looks up now, her eyes dry and angry. It looks painful. Tears would be better.

"Either one, I guess." I don't want to know, period. I guess I shouldn't have asked, then.

"I know she did it. I heard Marianne and Sandi talking when they didn't think I was around. When they talked to me, they tried way too hard to tell me it was this big accident. That she was just trying to cross the street and didn't see the giant truck coming toward her. But when they were talking to each other, they said different things. Like how she couldn't take it any more, and how maybe it was for the best because her life's so messed up and everything." Her head drops down again, and she's quiet for so long I wonder again if she's fallen asleep. I wait silently. I don't have any words for her. She starts talking again quietly, staring straight ahead at the wall.

"How could they say that stuff? How could they say she had nothing to live for and was better off dead? Who's better off dead? Just because she had some troubles with drinking and maybe some drugs and stuff? It's not like she was sick with cancer or something that couldn't be cured. She just needed to sober up. Not die. Do you think she's better off dead?" She looks directly at me, taking me off guard.

"I never even knew her."

"It doesn't matter! No one is better off dead unless they're dying of some horrible disease or something. No one is better off dead if they have a kid!" She covers her eyes with her hands, rubbing at her face like she's trying to take it off so she can start over again as someone else. I know the feeling.

"Maybe there was stuff in her life that you just don't know about." I don't have any idea what I'm talking about, but I feel like I have to say something.

"It doesn't matter what stuff was in her life! I was in her life. I'm her daughter! How could she think her life was so horrible if she had me? I mean, I know I wasn't living with her, but we were working on it. I still saw her. I was going to go back and live with her as soon as things worked out."

"I know."

"You know. I know. Why didn't she know? Why didn't she know that I need her? What am I supposed to do without a mother? Who's going to love me now?" Now the tears come. Loud and long and wet. She cries and cries. I sit kind of paralyzed. I don't know what to do with all that grief. I feel bad for her, but I can't fix it so I don't try. It seems to go on forever. I didn't know that there were that many tears in the human body.

"Alisha?" The door opens, and Buffy comes running in. She takes one look at me, with her usual "you're an idiot" look, and goes right over to Alisha's bed. She sits beside her and wraps her arms around her and kind of rocks her back and forth. She's muttering stuff to her that I can't really hear. I don't want to hear it, anyway. I've had enough of trying to be comforting and helpful for one night. I roll back toward the wall and put my pillow over my head to block out the sounds of Alisha crying for her mom.

I never cry for my mom. Of course, I don't know if she's alive or dead, so I guess there's not much to cry about. Far as I know, no one knew until a couple of years ago. Cecilia says I'm to tell her when I want my personal history because I'm old enough to deal with it. She's been saying that for a while. Nice of her to decide when I'm allowed to have the pieces of my own life. Not that I'm in any hurry to get them. I'm not sure I want to know. I'm not sure which would make me feel worse. Do I want to hear that she's alive and just decided to ditch me because she had better things to do with her time? Or do I want to hear she's dead?

It doesn't really matter much either way, does it. What do I need a mother for now, anyway? I'm fifteen years old, old enough to live on my own and take care of my own business. A mother would just get in my way.

chapter 17

"So, have you given any more thought to the testing?"

I'm sitting in the resource room again. Been spending lunch-time here most days. Beats the cafeteria or walking around outside feeling stupid. Besides, I'm getting kind of used to this computer thing. I actually did some homework yesterday without copying off anyone else. Still feels a bit like cheating, though, with the computer there reading to me and telling me what the words mean. Then again, copying off someone else could be considered cheating, too, I guess, though I still think it's easier to hide.

"What?" I have my earphones in and I'm actually listening to the world's most boring science chapter. Maybe this computer thing isn't so hot after all. At least before I didn't actually ever read the garbage at all. Now I get to hear every boring word.

"The testing I told you about earlier in the term. You remember. The psychometrist from the board office comes in for a day or so and does some testing of your learning profile. You wouldn't find it any tougher than what you and I did. More likely it will seem easier."

"This is working out OK for me. It's helping and all."

"That's great. I figured it would. But I'd still like to get a better picture of what's going on with your learning."

"What difference does it make? I don't think I want to know if I'm retarded or whatever." She kind of flinches when I say the word.

"I don't have any worries about your intellect. I just want to get a better handle on your learning style and what might be contributing to some of your difficulties."

"Difficulties like not being able to read or write. The unimportant crap, right?"

"Right." She laughs at me like she thinks I'm funny and looks at me like she actually likes me. Which of course she can't, because teachers hate me. It's a rule.

"The computer takes care of the reading, and you said you're going to show me some more stuff that'll help with the writing. That's all I need." Actually, it's more than I need, because I am going to get out of school and find a job the minute I can.

"Yes, but the testing will help you understand your own learning style better and will also give your teachers a better understanding of what you're all about. Once we know whether or not there's an actual learning issue, we can use the information to get you special accommodations and possibly even your own computer equipment. Although, that's only a maybe."

"I get my own computer just for being stupid? Cool."

"Ha, ha. I'm not even going to dignify that one with an answer. You know how I feel about that word." I actually do know how she feels about it. She seems to actually think that I'm not stupid. Which would be flattering and everything except that she also said that she doesn't think that any kid is stupid, and I know for a fact that there are all kinds of stupid kids out there. So I guess she's just a bad judge of stupidity.

"Anyway, Sadie. As I think I already told you, even though the decision is up to you as to whether or not you're willing to try the tests, I also need permission from your legal guardian. I have some forms that she or he would need to sign." She hands me an envelope. I look at it without taking it.

"I didn't say I was going to do it."

"I know. Just take the forms and if you decide you want to give it a try, talk it over with your guardian and get back to me. OK?"

"OK. I guess. But I still don't know why you're pushing this."

"Sorry if I seem pushy. I just think you have lots of untapped potential in there." She taps me on the top of the head. I brush her touch away, pretending I'm fixing my hair. "Kids who have identified learning needs can go to college and university and still get the help they need."

"What's that got to do with me?" College? University? Is she nuts? Number one, I'm the world's worst student; number two, I hate school; and number three...I hate school.

"You're a smart lady. I think there are all kinds of things you could do if we could get your learning style figured out."

"You're kind of a dreamer, aren't you?" She laughs and looks at me with that confusing "I like you" look again.

"I guess I have to be to do this job. Anyway, we'll talk more about it later. I have a couple of study skill features I want to show you today, so don't leave just yet. I'll be back in a few minutes."

I nod at her and sit at my computer like all the other speds. No one really talks to me here. A couple of the girls smile when I come in. Not a mean "ha-ha" smile like you'd expect, but just kind of a "hi" smile. No one seems to have taken an ad out in the local paper telling everyone that I'm part of the sped brigade, because no one's giving me a hard time about it outside of the room, either. Yet.

Nothing's really changed in class, though, except that sometimes I actually have my homework kind of done, and so I don't get ragged on by the teacher all of the time. There are computers in all of my classes, but they can just sit there at the back of the room and keep out of my face. There is no way I'm going back there in front of the whole class and sticking my little earphones in and giving everyone the chance to say things they'll regret. It's different in the resource room. I mean, what can the other speds say? They're all in there, too.

I don't know why Jackson is so set on testing my brain more. I don't think there's enough stuff in there to test, anyway. Mostly it's full of blank spaces with the occasional less-than-brilliant thought floating around looking for a place to land. There sure aren't enough of them in there to get me to college. Why would I want to do more school, anyway? I hate it. I just need to get through what they make me get through and then go out and get a job so I can get out of the fostergirl crap and just be a person.

Besides, I don't want to talk to my social witch about school. It's none of her business.

It's nobody's business. Just mine. I have no one to talk to about it, so I'll just figure it out on my own. Can't talk to Jackson 'cause she's the one who wants me to do it. Can't talk to Alisha 'cause she has her own problems and only talks about herself. Can't talk to Buffy 'cause I kind of hate her. Can't talk to the Ks 'cause they're just babies. Can't talk to Sandi 'cause it's none of her business how I do in school.

Can't talk to Rhiannon 'cause I blew her off. I blew her so far away that she'll never find her way back. Which is fine, because I don't need her and her charity-case friendship. Even though she says she wasn't trying to collect me and that she just wanted a friend because friends are hard for her to find.

Why would she have trouble finding friends? She isn't really a fostergirl, even if people have called her that. Kids with normal families and normal lives always have friends. Normal kids hang around long enough in one place to make friends and keep them. Rhiannon might spend too much time flapping her gums and thinking about the universe and trying to save the world, but she's basically a normal kid. Living with fosterkids doesn't make you into one. It's not something you catch like the flu.

Wonder what Rhiannon would tell me to do about this testing stuff? Not that I really care, but I bet she'd tell me to not worry about what the social witch thinks and to go for it. Get the stupid signatures and have the stupid test and find out that Jackson's wrong and that there are actually stupid kids out there after all.

chapter 18

I get to the top of my street and I see the car. I can't believe it! Why is the social witch here today of all days? Did Jackson call her so she could ambush me the minute I get home with the forms? I bet she did. Typical teacher. Acts all nice and supportive and tells me how I get to make the decision and then goes behind my back and calls my so-called guardian so they can talk about me and make my decisions for me, because she really thinks I'm just a stupid kid after all.

Well, they can't force me to do anything I don't want to do. I take the envelope Jackson gave me out of my bag and very carefully rip it into as many pieces as I can. I throw the pieces up in the air and they sprinkle down on my head like dry rain drops. I shake them out of my hair and then step on them a few times to grind them into the ground. There. Case closed.

There are a couple of other cars here, too, that I don't recognize. Maybe there's a party going on. Maybe all the workers and social witches are in the kitchen getting drunk and dancing on the table. Actually, probably not. They'd have to be human to do that.

"Sadie, is that you?" Sandi calls to me from the living room as I close the front door. Doesn't sound much like a party. I can hear people talking and something that sounds like crying. Great. Someone else died.

"Hi Sadie." Cecilia is sitting on the couch beside Sandi.

There's another woman I don't recognize in there, too. She smiles at me. I stare back at her.

"Hi."

"I guess you're wondering what's going on." Sandi looks at me with kind of sad eyes. Maybe her mom died.

"Not really."

"Well, we'll tell you anyway." Cecilia sits forward, looking like she's going to give me bad news. If she is about to tell me my mother died, I can save her the trouble. My mother died for me a long time ago.

"Sadie, the group home is closing and we have to find another place for all of you girls to live." Sandi says it fast, like she's tearing off a bandage. My so-called solid listening skills don't seem to be working. Sounded like she said that the group home is closing.

Not that it would be a big deal if it was. I just thought that a group home was different from a foster home. Like it was more stable or something. Foster homes always come and go. You never know when you might wake up in the morning with your suitcase open on the floor beside your bed so that you can get packing for the next pseudohome. But I sort of thought group homes were a permanent deal unless you messed up and got kicked out.

"What?"

"The group home is closing. We have to find you a new home." Cecilia's talking now.

"I heard that. I just don't really get it. How does it just close?"

"Well, it won't be overnight. We have a couple of weeks to get you all placed. But our funding was repealed and we were hoping that something could be worked out, but it didn't happen."

"So you knew this might be coming?" I look at Sandi. She kind of looks away.

"For a while."

"But you didn't think it was worth letting us in on the secret. Like it's none of our business, right? Who cares about a bunch of stupid fostergirls anyway, right? We're just like the pile of garbage out in the shed. Stick it in a bag and send it off to the dump. That's just great."

"Go Sadie." Everyone's head swivels toward the voice at the door. It's Buffy. She looks upset but kind of weirdly calm at the same time. She's usually one or the other, not both. Spooky.

"Come in, Buffy. We all need to talk about this." Sandi kind of waves her into the room. Buffy just shakes her head. The other lady stands up.

"Buffy, we do need to talk. We can go up to your room and discuss it privately if you would like." I guess that one is Buffy's social witch. Buffy looks at her and shakes her head again. I can't believe how quiet she is. If there was going to be a time for her to lose it, this would be it. But she doesn't. No yelling and screaming or freaking out. Nothing at all. Just shaking her head back and forth, like maybe she's trying to see things from a different angle.

"Do you know what they're doing?" Buffy stops shaking and is looking at me, making it clear to all the so-called grownups that she isn't including them.

"Besides sitting around? Nope."

"They're splitting up the Ks. That's the crying you can hear."

"Are you kidding me?" The kids who never had anybody and finally found each other are going to be split? Not that it surprises me, but it makes me sick, too.

"Buffy, Krista and Kendra's guardians will do what's best for them. Just as I will for you. This is rough on everyone." Buffy's worker sits back down. Buffy looks at her and shakes her head again. I'm still waiting for the fireworks, but when Buffy starts to talk, she's still calm and even makes sense.

"It's not rough for you. All you have to do is phone a few people and find somewhere else to dump me. Again. Not rough for the Ks' social workers. They just have to do the same thing and don't have to bother worrying about whether the Ks can survive on their own. Those kids totally depend on each other. They're like family. Not that any of us can remember what a real family is like." She stops talking and closes her eyes for a second. I'm still so amazed at how she's acting that I haven't even finished processing what she said. Great listening skills.

"This is not a good situation for anyone. We all just have to do our best." Cecilia this time. Opening her mouth and spouting sentences that don't mean anything. She does that a lot. I mean, I know on some level it's not her fault. It's not like she closed the group home or told all my pseudomoms to send me back to the kid store. I know that she's the one who's supposed to be on my side and looking out for me. I also know that she does that for like a gazillion kids and doesn't really have time to worry about just me. But I still agree with Buffy.

"Buffy is right. You don't have to do your best. You just have to pick up the phone. We're the ones who have to do our best.

Which is never good enough." More words falling out of my
mouth. I haven't talked this much for years. Scratch that. I haven't
ever talked this much in my life. If I don't stop, I'll start sounding
like Rhiannon...only the alternate universe version of her who
only says dark things.

"You people can just sit here and decide what happens next
in our lives and we have absolutely no control over it. I'm going
to see the Ks and try to help them feel better. Not that I'll be able
to say anything that will actually help." Buffy shakes her head
again. She must be getting dizzy by now. She heads toward the
Ks' room, where I can still hear some muffled crying sounds. Poor
kids. Not that I actually took the time to get to know them or
anything, but they seem all right to me. They keep to themselves
and out of everyone's hair. They have their own little world and
they don't need the rest of us. What's going to happen to them
now? Where will they end up?

Better question would be, what's going to happen to *me* now?
Where will I end up?

Standing there listening to them cry, my throat starts to ache a
little, and my eyes are stinging. What's the matter with me? I don't
cry. Especially just because some little kids are being separated. It's
not my problem. I have my own problems. But listening to them
bawling about having to say good-bye makes me feel lousy. Like
I know how they feel. Like I've felt it before. Which is just dumb.
I mean, I never cried when I left any of my pseudohomes. Why
would I? No one cries over losing fake families.

Don't know if I cried when they took me away from my
brother. Wonder why they did that, anyway? Why wouldn't they
have kept us together so we could at least have had someone to
jump around the foster system with? Wonder why I'm thinking

about the past when the future seems to have just gone down the toilet.

I look at the workers sitting there planning their phone calls. I don't want to ask them what happens next. I don't really care. I've run out of words, so I just do a Buffy and shake my head and go up to my room. Only I guess it isn't my room any more. Now I understand why they weren't in any great hurry to fill Charlene's bed when she disappeared. They already knew that the room was going to belong to a real person who belongs to a real family soon enough.

"Hey." Alisha is in there, looking a lot more cheerful than she has in a long time. Maybe the whole grieving thing is over with.

"Hey." I sit on my bed and put my head on my fists. I have a headache that feels like it is trying to punch its way out of my skull.

"So, guess the roommate thing's almost over. Wonder what they'll do with the house?" Alisha sounds as cheerful as she looks. Maybe she's gone totally nuts or something. Maybe I'll go there too. Seems like a happy place.

"You sound pretty happy about that. Guess we never really did get along that well." I'm talking down into my lap, but she hears me anyway.

"No, it's not that! We did OK. You were pretty cool when I freaked over my mom and all. And you never tried to kick the crap out of me like Buffy baby did about a hundred times."

"Buffy isn't always a total jerk, though. You have to admit she was pretty cool about your mom. Cooler than me."

"She gets points for that, I guess. But like I told you, she likes to help out when she thinks someone is weaker than her. I was pretty out of it for a while, and Buffy stepped up. But I feel better now, so she probably hates me again." Alisha doesn't look too upset at the idea.

"I can't believe how calm she is about the home shutting down and them splitting up the Ks. She's talking to everyone down there and even making sense." I sound like I'm defending her. I'd better watch it or I'll piss Alisha off, and we'll be the ones fighting.

"Yeah. Don't let it fool you. When she's beyond totally mad and freaked out, she gets all spooky and calm like that. She actually cares about those little kids, and she's got to be completely pissed about how they're being treated. Just wait. She'll probably knife someone in the middle of the night. She did it once before." She says it like it was something cool.

"Here?"

"No, her last place. I think it happened when they told her she was coming here. I don't think she actually used the knife. Just kind of waved it around or whatever. Anyway, enough about her. Guess what?"

"Gee, I don't know. The group home's closing and none of us has anywhere to live?"

"Oh, yeah. That sucks for you guys. But not for me!"

"What do you mean?"

"My nana is taking me!" I look at her big smile and think about her teeny tiny grandma. Man, this girl could swallow that woman in one gulp.

"You already know this?"

"Well, I guess on account of my mom and everything they were talking to her about the group home maybe closing. Anyway, she talked my aunt into moving in, too, so we're going to be like a chick family. Totally cool!" She does a little happy dance around the room.

"That's nice for you."

"It is, isn't it? I mean, I'm sorry for you guys and all. I've totally been there with the whole not-knowing-where-you're-going thing and all, and I'm trying to be sympathetic, but I'm too happy for myself to really think about it. Sorry!" She sure doesn't look sorry, but I guess I can't blame her. Going to an actual home must be somewhat cool. Kind of sucks that her mom decided to check out before her kid made it home, though.

My head is pounding through my fists. I really want to start pounding back, which would probably be a bad plan, so I get up and leave the room. Can't stay in there and watch Alisha dancing around and packing her bags. I think about going down and talking to Buffy and the Ks, but it seems like it would give me an even bigger headache than I already have. Besides, Buffy knows how to do all that comforting garbage. I'd just be in the way. So I just sit on the stairs and wish my head would fall off and roll away.

"So, what are her options?" I can hear Sandi's voice coming up from the living room. I don't want to hear it, but I don't have anything else to do, so I listen. Cecilia's voice coming at me like a cheese grater, shredding what's left of my brain.

"Well, we actually had a call this afternoon from a foster family right here. They have some space right now because one of their kids just had custody returned to her father. She'll be out within a week or two, which would work out just about right for Sadie."

I lean forward, trying to hear without being seen. They're down there discussing my life. I should go down and join, but I can't make myself do it. Which one will this be? Fourteen? Fourteen pseudohomes? Is that the right count? I try going back over it in my head, but it hurts. I know I stayed a few places for way less than a year. I've only been here three months. Now I have to go again because I'm only fifteen and can't get them to let me free.

Another set of pseudoparents. I thought that was all over with when I got in here. I mean, a group home is totally disgusting and bizarre, but at least it's not fake. No one pretends to be your parents or your sister or anything. It is what it is. A place to dump fostergirls who have outstayed their welcome in their fosterhomes. I can't believe I have to go back to one of those places. Knowing my luck, there'll be biokids who will totally resent me and want to make my life a bigger black hole than it already is.

"Oh, do you mean the Kerry house?" Sandi says, sounding pleased.

"Yes! Lily actually called and specifically asked about Sadie. I guess she's friends with her daughter."

My head has started to buzz, and I can't hear anything else they're saying.

Alisha was right all along. Rhiannon has finally done it. She's found a way to collect me.

She has her new fostergirl.

chapter 19

"No way."

"Sadie, it's a good solution."

"A good solution for you, maybe. Save you some phone calls." Four days and Cecilia hasn't even tried to find something different for me. Must be nice when other people do your job for you.

"This isn't about me. It's about you. You need somewhere to live. You're just getting settled in your new school, and this would let you stay."

"I don't care about school. I'll be sixteen in like two months. I can stay by myself."

"Sadie. We've had this talk. Very few kids are considered for emancipation as young as sixteen. As a matter of fact, the agency is considering changing that rule, so that it may not even be an option. Lots of other agencies don't consider sixteen-year-olds for independent living."

"I'm not with lots of other agencies. I'm with this one. I want to go it alone."

Cecilia looks at me and kind of sighs. She folds her arms and shakes her head, like she can't figure out what to say. Which I know isn't true, because she knows exactly what to say. She's said it a dozen times or a hundred times. I don't know how many, but I know what the words are. I'm too big a mess and too stupid to go it alone, and she has the right to tell the people who make those decisions that I'm not ready. She feels she has a duty to be honest and doesn't want to set me up for failure…blah blah blah.

"I know you want to try. And I know from your face that you know the answer. Sadie, maybe in a few months things will be different, but we need something for you right now. You're not even sixteen yet, so this isn't even a discussion we can have. Ultimately, you don't have a choice here, but I thought it would be best for everyone if there was some kind of agreement."

"Some kind of agreement. You mean the kind where all the adults agree about what is best for me and I have to do it or else get locked away somewhere."

"Sadie. No one is locking you away anywhere. Your probation term is up soon and you haven't breached any of the conditions. There are no grounds for recommending a more secure placement. You know all of this."

"All I know is I'm being dumped into another house where no one wants me and where I don't want to be." I sound whiney. I don't want to sound whiney. I'm not whining. I'm just tired of it.

"But that's not the case. The Kerrys specifically asked if you could come and stay with them. I went over there yesterday and spoke with Mrs. Kerry at length. I think this will work out for you, Sadie. They're good people, and they make a long-term commitment to their kids."

"*Their* kids. Hardly."

"That's how they see it. The Kerrys don't just see this as a job. They see it as their lifestyle. They love having lots of young people around. I'm sure you know that they have adopted some of their foster children. They keep in touch with every child who has come through their doors, no matter how long they actually lived with them."

"Sounds like a TV movie. A pukey one."

"Well, pukey or not, it's the reality of this particular home. It's our best choice right now."

"It's *your* best choice. I don't have a choice."

"If you are dead set against it, I can try to find something else. But it will likely mean a temporary placement until I can find somewhere more permanent for you."

"Whatever." I close my eyes for a second. I can't think straight about this. Not that I can think straight about much of anything. I don't know what to do. I hate the temporary homes. I mean, they're *all* temporary, but the ones where they know you're only there for a few weeks are the worst. No one even tries to pretend you belong. They're not even fake parents in those places. They're just putting up with you for the money until they can get rid of you.

I can't live on my own because the social witch has no faith in me. The group home is history. Can I stand being a part of Rhiannon's collection? Is it a collection? Is Alisha right or is Rhiannon telling it straight? Who do I believe? Who do I trust?

I don't believe anyone. I don't trust anyone. I don't have anyone. There's just me. I have to look out for me. I just don't know how to do that right now.

Even in my own head I sound like a totally pathetic whiner. Man, I have to stop this and just make a decision. Cecilia's standing there looking at me with big sympathetic cow eyes. I must really be a basket case, 'cause usually she's just pissed with me when I make her life difficult.

The room is ridiculously quiet. I can almost hear my own brain creaking as it tries to make a decision. I can hear Cecilia breathing. I can almost hear her brain clicking into gear, too, though I know she's already made a decision.

Screw it.

"Fine. I'll go live with the stupid Kerrys. I'm sure they'd love to have me in their perfect little family. It'll be wonderful." I say this with my eyes closed still. I don't want to see the happy look on the cow's face.

"I'm glad. I know you're being sarcastic, but it just might turn out to be wonderful. I'll go over there and let them know."

My eyes stay closed until she leaves. Maybe I'll keep them closed forever, along with my mouth. Maybe I'll get a set of earplugs, too. I can just sit in the corner at Rhiannon's house, and then I won't have to hear them, see them, or talk to them.

I go upstairs to my so-called room where my soon-to-be-former roommate is cheerfully packing. I try to leave again before she sees me, but it doesn't work.

"Sadie! Where're you going? You should get started packing!"

"Yeah, right. I have one knapsack and one duffel bag that I throw my junk into. It takes about thirty seconds. Better get right on that."

"Oh. Well, I'm doing it now because I could be going any day. My aunt is just getting a few details figured out and then I'm history!"

"Sounds good." She does sound good. It's weird how happy she is. It's like she's totally over her mom, and all is right with the world now. I kind of figured that losing a parent, a real one, would make someone sad for a long time. Like they'd walk around looking all droopy eyed and wouldn't smile and would just look for a corner to hide in until the pain went away. That's what I think I'd do. If I had anyone real to be sad about. There I go, whining again. What is with me? I need my brain to totally shut up.

"It is good. I mean, I wish like crazy that my mom was going to be there, too, but she would want this for me. She would be totally happy that things worked out this way. Except for the part about her not being there, that is." Yeah, except for that part. A pretty big part, if you ask me. Not that anyone would ask my opinion when it comes to mothers. Or anything else.

"Anyway, glad it's worked out for you. Gotta go." Not sure where I have to go to, but I know I have to get out of this room. I wander down the hall toward Buffy's room. She isn't going to be happily packing from what I hear. Her social witch found her another group home in another city. New school. New fake friends. At least she won't have to deal with fake parents.

"Hi." I stand in the doorway. I don't make it a habit to drop in on Buffy, so I figure it's safest to keep my distance. She's not packing. She's just sitting.

"Hi." She looks at me. Her eyes are kind of shiny, like she wants to cry but can't. I think about making a quick retreat, but something makes me stand there. She looks really alone, sitting there all curled up in her chair. She's hugging herself around the knees and just kind of staring at me like she wants me to do something. I don't know what.

"Um, so, Alisha's packing and everything. She seems happy." I take a step into the room and lean against the wall. Buffy doesn't move.

"Yeah. I guess I'm happy for her. I hope it works out this time."

"This time?"

"Yeah. Her aunt did step up once before and take her in a few years ago. Her mom was in rehab or jail or something at the time. Anyway, it didn't work out. Not sure why they're letting it happen again. She gets her hopes up, and then they have farther to fall." She's still just staring. I'm not even sure I saw her blink.

"That sucks."

"Does it? At least she gets a chance to have her hopes up for a while. I think I'd go for that. Going to another dumb-ass group home isn't exactly a hope builder."

"No, I guess not. You'll have to teach them all the rules." She looks at me and almost smiles for a second. Almost.

"Yeah. If they're as stupid as all you guys, it'll take a while." Her head goes down on her knees. When she looks up again, one tear has escaped her shiny eyes and is rolling down her cheek. I stare at it, watching it drip off her chin onto her sweater. My eyes sting for a second, like they want to join in, but I will it away. Tears don't solve anything.

"You'll get them in line. You're pretty scary." This time she actually smiles, but it's a sad smile bisected by another tear.

"Thanks. I hear you're probably going to Rhiannon's."

"I guess. Not much choice."

"You're lucky. I know kids who have lived there. It's supposed to be OK there."

"Yeah. So I've heard."

"Seriously. Rhiannon is actually OK. I mean, she's weird and all that, but that kind of makes her more OK, you know? She's not full of herself and everything."

"No. She's just a collector."

"A collector? Oh, you mean that crap Alisha fed you? Don't listen to her. She totally loved it there when she lived there. She told me. She just got bent about the fact that they couldn't take her back later. If she wasn't going to her aunt's she'd probably be fighting you for the spot there now. I wish I was going there." That seems pretty unbelievable to me, but she looks too down to be up to lying.

"I'll let you know if another spot comes up."

"Oh, sure. 'Cause you really loved living with me, right? It's been so wonderful here at MacAvoy where everyone gets along." She shakes her head.

"It's been OK. Not wonderful, but OK. I guess. Maybe." She looks at me and actually laughs.

"Don't get too mushy, here, Sadie. Wouldn't want me to think you had, like, a feeling in there or anything."

"No, feelings make life too complicated. I do better without them. Anyway, guess I should go and do something. Homework or jump off a bridge or whatever."

"They're about the same."

"Totally." I stand there for a second, not sure how to say good-bye to her. She looks kind of small sitting there, tears making her shrink into her chair. I wonder if she wants a real hug or something. I only wonder it, though. I don't do hugs. I just kind of do a wave thing and walk out. She doesn't wave back because her head is back down on her knees. She doesn't even notice I'm gone.

I won't go down to see the Ks. I never took the time to get to know them. I don't have anything to say to them now. Actually, it's not a them anymore. Kendra is already gone to another home. Krista sits in her room and doesn't talk to anyone. I don't even know what they have planned for her. All I know is it won't be with Kendra.

I don't remember how I felt when I was alone with my first pseudofamily. I don't remember missing my brother or my mother. Maybe I was too small and stupid. Maybe I just didn't care. Wonder if my brother ever missed me. Can't remember anyone ever missing me. Mostly they've just been happy to see me go.

I should go over to Rhiannon's and talk to her mom about the big decision that I guess I made. I should figure out when I'm moving in and where I'm going to sleep. I should figure out how I'm going to face Rhiannon when she sees me for the first time as her new "fostersister" instead of just her former useless friend.

I should figure out what I'm going to do with the rest of my life.

I should do my homework.

Maybe I should just find that bridge.

chapter 20

"Well, I am very glad to hear that you're not leaving school. I think we have more work to do together." Jackson gives me a big smile like everything is fantastic in her universe. Nice for her.

"More work. Oh, good. This just keeps on getting better." I don't even know why I came here to tell her. I've been avoiding Rhiannon all morning, which was hard to do because we had science first period today, and she looked at me like she expected us to have a chat, and I had to pretend to be really concentrating on my book so that I wouldn't make eye contact and accidentally talk to her. The resource room just seemed like a good place to hide, I guess.

"Well, I think you're really doing a great job with the tech we've tried so far. I really want to get you going on the writing program. And I still want you to think about the testing."

"I have enough to think about right now, thanks."

"I can imagine that you do. I don't know what you're going

145

through at all, but I can also imagine that it's pretty tough being uprooted every time you turn around. Unbearably tough. I admire your strength."

"You what?" She admires my strength? What's her angle? Does she want me to move some furniture for her or something?

"I admire your strength. You're a tough lady and I think you have a remarkably strong sense of yourself in a situation where that should be almost impossible."

"Sure. Whatever." Lame answer but I can't think of anything else to say. I've never had an adult tell me she admires me before. I don't think I've had anyone tell me they admire me. Except guys who want to admire me on my back.

"Yeah, whatever. I'm not trying to embarrass you. I just wanted you to know that I think you're a good kid who's had an impossible life. I grew up in one house with one set of parents, and I still had all kinds of trouble figuring out who I was or where I was going."

"Yeah, well, you're probably the only one who would call me a good kid. I'm no angel."

"I'm not a big fan of angels. At least not in my classroom."

"You are one weird lady."

"So I've heard. So, have you talked to Rhiannon or her mother yet about the move?" I look around the room to make sure no one is listening. It's the usual geek squad in here today, most of them with headphones on at the computers or their MP3s blaring in their ears at the desks.

"No. Not ready for that yet."

"Oh, I thought you'd be excited to get organized. Ms. Kerry is a lovely woman and Rhiannon is a sweetheart. I thought you two were friends."

"No. I blew that one. It's a talent of mine."

"I'm sorry to hear that. Rhiannon's a good kid and would make a good sister."

"Foster sister."

"OK. A good foster sister. Either way, whatever happened between you, I'm sure you can work it out."

"I'm not so good at working stuff out in the friend department. Never had much time for it. Always seemed like too much of a hassle. Now I know it is."

"Most things that are worth anything come with some work."

"I've heard that one before. Mostly from teachers trying to get me to do my homework." She laughs. She laughs at me a lot. I don't usually put up with people laughing at me, but Jackson does it differently. She isn't making fun. She actually thinks I'm funny. In a good way.

"I guess it does sound like teacher talk. But it really is true. And friends are certainly work, but they're one of those work things that are worth the effort. Most of the time, anyway."

"What about the rest of the time?"

"Some friends turn out to be something different from what you thought."

"Yeah." The bell rings, which is a good thing because this chat's turning into some sort of guidance session. That Jackson's tricky. I grab my bag and head out the door, thinking about our conversation. Because I'm looking inside my head instead of outside, I run into the first person I meet out in the hall. Rhiannon.

"Hi Sadie."

"Hi." I keep walking. I want to talk to her but I don't have any idea what to say. Rhiannon used to fill in any gaps that I leave, but that was when we were friends…or whatever.

"So, my mom told me that you might be coming to live with

us." She's using the quiet version of her voice. Maybe she doesn't want anyone to know about this, either.

"Your mom told you?" I look at her for a second. Why would her mom have to tell her anything? I mean, I figured the whole thing had been her idea in the first place.

"Yes. She heard about the group home closing and she knew we were going to have space. She likes you and she thought it would be good for you to stay here for school and everything. So, she called the agency and suggested you come live with us. Then she talked to your social worker and told her she wanted you to come to our place and I guess they both decided it was a good idea."

"Your mom likes me?" First Jackson, now Rhiannon's mom? Am I losing my edge?

"Yeah. Everyone in my house likes you."

"Everyone?" I look at her again. We're almost to my classroom so I stop walking.

"Yes, everyone!" She sounds kind of pissed, which is not what I was expecting. "Including me. Even though you are stubborn and pigheaded and not too bright in the friend department. I don't know why you listened to Alisha instead of me. Maybe she's a better friend to you or something but you *are* allowed to have more than one friend and when you're friends with someone and you think something is up, you don't just dump them and run off hiding in some corner somewhere. You talk to them and find out what's going on and if you do that maybe you find out that you were wrong and that the person is really just your friend. I told you I just want to be your friend. I told you that I don't collect foster kids or whatever it was that Alisha said. My house is already full of foster kids. I don't need to run out to collect more."

She stops for breath and looks at me. Yep, she's definitely pissed.

"So now I'll be helping to fill it up even more."

"Yeah, you will. And if it wasn't you, it would be someone else. Some other stranger coming into my house and my room. Some other person I have to get to know and try to like and share my family with. At least I already know you and I even like you although sometimes I have no idea why because you really make it hard to do." I look at her in surprise. Not exactly Suzy Sunshine today. It never occurred to me that she might find it tough having kids coming into her house all the time. I guess it should have. I mean, she has a family and parents and everything and still has to always wonder what's coming next. She doesn't know when those kids are coming or going. She has to deal with sharing her mom with kids who aren't even her biosibs. And if what she told me last time is true, she even has to deal with numb brains bugging her about being in a foster home. Even if she isn't the fostergirl.

"Ms. Thompson, are you planning on gracing us with your company? Ms. Kerry, I believe you have a class also. Somewhere." Wilson is standing in the door looking down his nose at us. I really, really, really want to stick a pencil up it and see if it disappears into his empty skull, but I resist the temptation.

"Yes, Mr. Wilson. Sir." I salute him, which makes his big nose turn red, and will probably make my next seventy-five minutes suck even more than they were already going to. But it also makes Rhiannon giggle, which is worth it.

"Yes, Mr. Wilson. Sir." Rhiannon salutes him, too, and then takes off down the hall. I open my mouth to say something to her back, but I can't figure out what I should say. I guess maybe "sorry" would cover it. I don't usually do sorry, but I suppose there's always a first time.

I guess there's a first time for lots of things. Like the first time that someone actually asked to have me come live with them. Like they actually want me around. Like they had a choice and they chose me.

The only problem now is figuring out how to actually go live with these people who think they want me around and not do something totally stupid that will make them regret it.

chapter 21

"So, my mom suggested putting us together in the same room because she has this theory that we're going to be talking about stuff and going into each others' rooms all the time anyway, which would bug the other person in the room, so it's just easier to start off this way in the first place. I could have had Shelly's spot but I like Mom's idea better so Chandra's going to take Shelly's spot which is OK with her. I kept my old bed if that's OK with you and put you on the other side where Chandra was. The sheets are all clean and everything which I know because I washed them myself because I've been doing the laundry for Mom for years. You'd be surprised at how much laundry all these kids make but I don't mind except when I have to iron. Do you like to iron?"

And she's back. Rhiannon in full talking form. I never even had to actually tell her that I'm sorry. She just decided we're friends again, and that she's all excited about me coming here and that's it. Nice to be able to just switch it on and off like that. I'm trying to feel comfortable with her and this room and this house and this situation. I'm trying not to think about Buffy crying as she walked to the car heading to her new group home, and Alisha skipping out to the car as she headed to her aunt's. I'm trying not to think about the Ks sitting alone in their new homes, hiding in their turtle shells until they find someone else who gives a crap about them.

This thinking-about-people thing is a hassle. I used to just shut them out. I never worried about the other kids in the houses I was dropped into. I don't know why I'm doing all of this think-ing now, but I don't like it and it needs to stop. It hurts my head and makes my eyes sore.

Rhiannon's looking at me like it's my turn to talk. Now I know we're back. I never know when I'm supposed to talk, or what she wants me to say. Did she ask me something? Something about laundry?

"Sure. Whatever."

"Seriously? Well, maybe that can be your job then because I hate it. Everyone around here has to contribute whatever they can, except the little guys of course because they're, well, little guys. Little girls, I mean. Anyway, I hope you don't mind that Mom stuck you in here with me. I know you think that I talk all of the time and will drive you nuts because I drive everyone nuts but I really can be quiet when you want me to and I'm a good sleeper so I won't be bugging you all night long. As far as I know, I don't talk in my sleep, though Mom says it wouldn't surprise her if I did!" She laughs at herself. I smile at her. It's impossible not to sometimes. Man, I hope she doesn't talk in her sleep!

I had my thirty seconds' worth of stuff unpacked before she even finished talking about the laundry and spent the time during the second speech looking around the room. The room is nicer than the one at MacAvoy. Rhiannon's side of the room looks the same as it did last time I was here. Books and clothes piled everywhere. I guess it looks like she tried to tidy it up a bit. Her mom probably made her. My side is totally cleaned out. There's a desk with nothing on it, with a shelf sitting above it waiting for books that aren't going to come any time soon. The bed looks comfortable and sits right under a window. It has a big, fluffy-looking comforter on it that looks like it would keep me warm outside in the middle of winter. There's a big closet for clothes at the far end that Rhiannon must have really spent some time clearing out, because half of it is empty. My stuff will take up about a quarter of the half. I guess that would be an eighth. Fostergirl math skills.

"This was actually supposed to be the master bedroom, which would have been my mom and dad's room, but they decided that they didn't need all this space as much as I do, because I have to share so often with the kids who come in, so they actually sleep in a really small room. Mom doesn't care because she says she has a whole house to live in and what does she need a great big room for anyway and that teenagers need space more than old ladies do. Not that she's an old lady, but she likes to call herself that, mostly I think so that we will tell her she isn't old at all. My computer works pretty well and you can use it whenever you want. You can put the rest of your stuff away in the closet if you want to and then we can go downstairs to see if Mom wants any help with supper."

"My stuff is already all away." Rhiannon looks over at the closet and then at me.

"We definitely have to get you more stuff. I have lots of stuff which you can borrow whenever you want except that our styles are pretty different, aren't they? We are also completely different sizes so I guess that won't work but maybe sweaters because they stretch. You mostly do the sweatshirt thing though and I have all these knit sweaters that my grandma makes me because she likes to knit and I'm her only grandchild. She doesn't knit much for the other kids because she isn't all that cool with the idea that Mom brings so many other kids into the house but doesn't have any other bio kids that Grandma can call her real grandchildren, even though it isn't Mom's choice. Mom and her used to argue about it when she came to visit and they thought I wasn't listening. She doesn't come here much any more, but I go see her. It's too bad they fight over something so lame. The funny part is she ends up knitting for everyone anyway because I always pass my sweaters down to whoever needs one and so there're kids all over the place wearing Grandma's sweaters. I'd give you one, but she likes bright colors, which wouldn't be your thing at all, would it?"

"No. But thanks. You said something about helping your mom?" By this point I'm not sure what she said, but I think it was something about supper. This is something I can do. Everywhere I can remember living, I've had all kinds of so-called "chores" to do. Setting tables and doing dishes and all that fun stuff might make me feel less like that chick Alice when she fell down a hole and disappeared into crazy land.

"Oh, right! We have to go now, too, or she'll end up doing it all by herself, which will not go over well." She runs out the door. I follow behind her, not quite so fast, because I'm kind of feeling my way. I've walked down this hallway more than once before. I've gone down these stairs and even worked in the kitchen to help get ready for supper. But that was when I was just visiting for a couple of hours. Now I live here, and it all looks different to me.

I'm still a visitor in someone else's house, but now I have to stay here and sleep here and wake up here and eat breakfast and have showers and use the bathroom.

By the time I'm at the bottom of the stairs, Rhiannon has made it into the kitchen where she's already babbling to her mom at three thousand miles an hour. I can see them through the doorway, like they're a moving picture in a frame. Rhiannon's mouth is going nonstop and her mom is smiling while she listens and gets food organized. Her dad isn't here yet. The living room is empty at the moment. It probably isn't empty very often. The kids must be down in the playroom or up in their rooms. I can't even remember how many live here.

There are some actual pictures in frames sitting on a shelf beside where I'm standing. Rhiannon at different ages. It looks like she's having a really hard time sitting still in every picture, and it feels like she's going to start talking at me. There are pictures there of other kids, too. I recognize Adam and another one of the girls whose name has totally left my head. There are a couple of pictures of her parents with various kids, too. Everyone's posed to look happy.

There aren't any pictures of me anywhere sitting on a shelf. I don't know what I looked like when I was a little kid. No one else does either, I guess. I suppose there were pictures taken of me at school when they managed to force me into the gym on picture day, but no one ever bought them. Why would they? So they could remember me after I was gone?

Wonder if there were pictures of me and my brother when we were really little. Before my mom disappeared. Smiling and looking happy and pretending to be a family. I can't imagine it. I don't even remember what he looked like. Weird to think I could walk right past him on the street and not even know who he is. He's like, seventeen or something now? Even if I did remember him, he'd look totally different.

I stay in the room for just a minute, breathing in the quiet space. I know that there won't be much quiet here. I usually can't stand noisy houses and little kids, and I have no idea how I'm going to survive it here. Rhiannon's pretty determined that she's going to make it work, which might actually drive me the rest of the way to crazy.

"Sadie! Did you get lost?"

"Coming!"

Everyone materializes out of nowhere for supper time and everything looks exactly the same as it did when I came here for supper as a "guest." The little wee kids are still talking with food coming out of their mouths and whining for more and spilling everything every two minutes, and Rhiannon's parents are still all cool and calm with it. Chandra's there, and even though she isn't saying much to me, she doesn't seem pissed I kicked her out of her room. Not sure where she ended up, but obviously still somewhere in the house. Hope she isn't stuck with the two little she-devils, 'cause that would definitely come back and bite me in the butt when she decides to claim her old spot back. Adam is there, too, all smiles and full of stories about his school day. He makes school sound like the greatest place on earth. Maybe I should totally check his school out. I mean, Jackson's pretty sure I have all kinds of specialness about me, too. Adam and I could ride the bus together.

The noise around this table is crazy and enough to ruin my appetite. The good part of it is still the same as the first time I came here, though. Everyone is so wrapped up in babbling

and wiping stuff up and stuffing their faces that no one is too
bent about the fact that I am keeping my mouth shut. It's weird,
though. I don't feel invisible here like I always have in other places
I've stayed. Even though no one is talking at me, every once in a
while Rhiannon's mom looks my way and smiles. One of the little
wee kids even stuck her fork into my potatoes and had a bite or
two before Rhiannon's dad made her stop. He smiles at me, too,
and kind of shrugs his shoulders as he tries to tell the kid to eat
off her own plate. The kid, I think her name's Mary or Marie or
something, just kind of laughs at him and then sticks her fork in
his potatoes and has a big bite with butter all dripping down her
chin. What a total brat! I wait for the fireworks to begin, and the
kid to be sent to her room.

"That's enough, Marie."

That's it. Three words from Rhiannon's mom and the kid
stops. It's something in the voice. You just know she's the boss.
Then again, maybe it's not just the voice at all. Maybe she knocks
them around a little when no one's looking, so she can keep them
in line the rest of the time. I had a fostermom who used to do
that. She was all calm and in control when anyone was around
and the minute she was alone with us the slapping started. She
didn't hit hard enough to leave marks. She just hit a lot, and it got
annoying, and we would behave ourselves just to make her stop.
Wonder if she's still in the business of hurting kids? Not that I
care, but I'd kind of like to catch her in the act now that I'm bigger
than her and slap her back. No, that wouldn't work. I'd just get in
crap. I know, I'll catch her in the act and film it. Not that I have a
camera or anything, but I'm sure Rhiannon, my new fostersister,
could find me one.

"Sadie?" Rhiannon is looking at me like I'm a little nuts.

I guess I was spacing out just when she decided to talk at me. Timing is everything.

"Yeah?" I kind of blink my eyes like I'm just waking up. The little kid who stole my food giggles. I glare at her and she stops.

"I asked you if you want to help clear and we'll grab dessert." She's already standing up with two plates in her hands. Chandra was already heading to the kitchen with a stack. I jump up, banging the table, making the little kid laugh again.

"Sure." I head into the kitchen with the two of them, arms loaded up with food and plates. I take too much because I'm trying to be helpful, I guess, and manage to drop everything on the floor just as I step into the kitchen. Gross leftover food everywhere. Unbelievable. What a dweeb! Great start.

"Sorry!" Not my favorite word, but the only one I can use at the moment. I crouch down and start picking up the mess, keeping my eyes on the floor so I don't have to see all the disgusted faces.

"No worries! We only use plastic around here. Too many little kids to use the good china, except when Grandma comes, which is almost never like I told you. I drop stuff all the time. Well, not all the time because I didn't today but I guess it was your turn today because this is quite a big mess, which only happened because you were trying too hard to help and carried too much stuff. I only carry two plates at a time. It takes longer but it doesn't really take longer because I drop less so I have to clean up less."

"Rhiannon, less talk, more helping," Mr. Kerry's voice calls out from the dining room. Chandra starts laughing as she drops down to the floor to help Rhiannon and me pick up the rest of the mess. I look at the two of them, who should be royally pissed that I made them crawl around on the floor. They're both grinning away and picking up disgusting bits of chicken and potato, some of which I'm pretty sure was already chewed up by one of the superbrats.

Day One.

Mess One.

It would be really nice if I didn't make any more messes while I'm here.

What are the odds?

chapter 22

"So, now that you're staying for a while, will you think about it?"

"Think about what?" As if I don't know.

"I know you think I'm being really pushy, Sadie. And I guess I am. I just feel strongly that we might find out some interesting and important information if you do the next level of testing. It'll only take a couple of sessions, and it happens here at school."

"Right. And it will be so much easier than the stuff I did with you. Which, by the way, was not fun."

"I know you're mocking me here, but it really could feel easier for you, at least parts of it."

"If it's so easy, why bother?"

"Well, maybe I exaggerate the case a little bit. It'll be like any test. You'll be pushed until it gets challenging, so we know what your limits are."

"Well, that shouldn't take very long then."

"I said that wrong. I meant, so we know what your abilities are."

"Still shouldn't take very long."

"Then you'll do it? If your worker signs the forms, which I'm sure she will."

"I didn't say that! I don't know. I just think it'll be a waste of time."

"Why don't we try this? I'll send another set of the forms and an explanation to Ms. Kerry, and you can talk it over with her before we go any further with it. I know she can't do the signing, but she can at least talk to you about it. You feel comfortable talking to her, don't you?"

"I never really tried talking to her about much. We say 'good morning' and 'hi' and 'how was your day' kind of thing. I don't spill my guts to her or anything. Even if I wanted to, there wouldn't be time. Too many other mouths flapping at her all the time." I'm not sure I want to get in Ms. Kerry's face. She's always so calm and in control of everyone that I'm pretty sure some day she's just going to completely blow her top. I don't want to be the one to set her off with something as lame as this.

"You've been living there now for about two, or is it three, weeks? Long enough to at least give Ms. Kerry a chance."

"I don't really know. Maybe. I can maybe talk to her. Though I still think it's all fine now. I mean, I'm doing a bit better in some of my classes, and I can even do some of Wilson's stuff on the computer here. Actually, it's a lot better than before."

"I'm really glad you feel that way. And none of that will change. This can't make things worse. Only better."

"Whatever. Give me the stuff for Ms. K, and I'll see if I can squeeze in between Rhiannon and the superbrats for a minute or two with her." 'Ms. K' is the name we came up with for me to call her. She told me to use her first name, same as I've done at most places, but when I tried calling her Lily it just didn't feel right. Maybe because I knew her first as Rhiannon's mom and called her Ms. Kerry. Now that I live there, "Ms. Kerry" seemed a bit formal, so we compromised.

"Are you still finding the little ones a bit much?"

"That's what you call an understatement. Man, they're crazy. Rhiannon thinks they're totally cute and can't wait to get home to see them every day. I just think they're loud and messy and out of their little minds."

"You were little like that once too, you know."

"I don't remember being that little. And if I was that bratty, it explains why my mom took off and left me." As soon as the words pop out of my mouth I try to bite them back. I don't ever talk about this stuff. To anyone. Not opening that door. Especially with a sneaky guidance babe like Jackson.

"Sadie, I…"

"No. Pretend I didn't say anything. I don't want to talk about it, so don't get that whole guidance face on. I have work to do." I put my ear buds in so I can shut out the world and listen to a robot voice read Shakespeare. To be or not to be? Good question.

Two weeks, four days. That's how long I've been at the Kerrys'. It's different there from anywhere else I've ever stayed. I don't know exactly what it is, though. From the outside looking in, it looks the same as lots of places I've been. I've been in other houses where people were relatively decent. It's not like all of my pseudomoms slapped me around or anything. Some of them were OK and even kind of nice to me. Lots of the other places were full of kids and noise just like this one. I always had to share a room with someone I barely knew.

Sometimes I think I remember sharing a room with my brother a hundred years ago. I have this foggy memory of *Toy Story* blankets and a Buzz Lightyear that used to say weird things when I was trying to sleep. Last time I saw him, I think I was three or something. Not sure. Truth is I'm not even sure I know what his name is. Or was. Sometimes kids' names get changed when they go into the system. Seem to half-remember him being called Chris but I'm not even sure that the memory is real. My brother is more of an idea than a reality to me. An idea that I don't have very often. I wonder if he's sharing a room with anyone now, and if they changed his name to Buzz?

I never shared a room before with anyone like Rhiannon, though, that's for sure. I had kind of thought that after a few days of living together, she would be starting to get sick of me and her happy-chirpy-excited routine would wear off. What's that saying? Something about familiarity and contempt? Anyway, two weeks, four days later and she's still talking my ear off every night and seems pretty happy every morning that I'm still there. Though I'm pretty sure she would be just as happy if there was a new flower pot in her room that she got to see every morning.

It's not just Rhiannon that makes it different, though. It's more of a feeling I get. I can't really describe it, even to myself. It's like they were all expecting me and aren't surprised that I'm there. It's like I've been there for a while and I'm just part of the crowd. I don't know. I need to stop thinking about it now.

"Mom will totally talk to you about it. I'll take Marie and Hillary out of the way and watch a movie with them or something. I don't have much homework so I can take the time. Mom's really good at figuring out big stuff like this. Although, if you want my opinion, which you probably don't, I would go for it. I think you're super smart and I think the tests will show that to everyone. I mean, being smart isn't just about reading and writing, and besides that's getting better anyway with all the computer stuff you have in Jackson's room. Hey, I wonder if we can get all that stuff here on my computer? That would be awesome and then you could do your homework at home instead of trying to get it done at lunchtime in Jackson's room and you can come back to the cafeteria so I don't have to eat with Sarah Smithson, who has braces and always has food in them."

"You could always come to Jackson's room instead."

"Oh, I don't think so."

"Why?"

"Oh, I don't know. I just don't really fit in there." She looks uncomfortable.

"Fit in? No one fits in there. It's not like a club or something. It's a classroom where kids work."

"Well, I don't need…I mean I don't use…I mean…" Her face is turning red and she seems to be having trouble talking, which means she's either dying of some dreadful disease or trying to hide something.

"You mean, you're not a *sped*." I can feel my feet starting to move faster like they're trying to get away from her. Didn't figure Rhiannon for a school snob, but I should have. She might talk too much and have trouble focusing sometimes, but she's actually smart and likes to read and do her homework.

"No, I don't mean that! Well, I guess I kind of do mean that, but not in the way you think."

"How do you know how I think? I'm just a stupid sped who can't think at all!" My feet are really moving now, and she has to jog to keep up.

"You know I don't think you're stupid. This isn't about you at all."

"Hey, I'm the sped who has to have even more tests to see how speddy I am."

"You're not a sped. I don't even really know what that means. It's just a stupid word that means nothing except that some stupid people have nothing better to do with their time than to make fun of other people." She's kind of panting, trying to keep up with me and talk to me at the same time. Hope she hyperventilates.

"So, what's your problem then?" I don't look at her, but I can hear her breathing behind me.

"First of all, I have enough problems with people calling me names because everyone thinks I'm weird and I don't need sped on top of everything else. So I guess I'm just a coward. And second of all, there's a guy." Her voice started out loud but died down so much by the last word that I'm not a hundred percent sure I heard her. I stop walking and look at her to make sure she hasn't passed out or something. Not really interested in doing CPR in the middle of the sidewalk.

"No one actually calls me sped." She stops walking, too, and glares at me for a minute before talking. She takes a deep breath and blows it out in my face.

"Yeah, well, that's because people know you're tough. You just have this 'don't mess with me' aura going on. I am not tough. I have a 'mess with me if you want to have a good time' aura going on. I would love to get rid of that particular aura but it seems to like me. Maybe you could loan me some of yours."

"I don't know anything about auras. You can have mine if you want."

"Thanks. Wish it was that easy. Anyway, I'm sorry if I sound like a snob or something. I'm totally not. I'm just a wuss. I really can't handle another name." She looks really bent out of shape about the idea.

"Fair enough. Didn't you say something else? Something about a guy?"

"Yeah. I guess. Maybe I said that there's a guy in there." She's looking down and turning even redder, which is kind of scary, because she's already outshining the fire hydrant.

"There's a few guys in there."

"Yeah, but one of them is Eddy Jameson."

"I'll take your word for it."

"He's in my English class and he's the cutest guy on the planet and he doesn't know I'm alive and he goes to Jackson's room because he likes to get extra computer time even though he uses the one in our class to do that program you use, you know, the one that reads stuff. He looks really cute with his headphones on, like he's a pilot or something, but I never said that to him of course because that would be lame, but anyway I couldn't go into Jackson's class because then he might think I'm following him. And Grace Miller and her friends would have a new name to call me and I really don't want them to have any more ammunition."

She looks at me like she thinks I understand what she's talking about.

"Who's Grace Miller and do you want me to take her out?"

"Take her out where?"

"To dinner at McDonald's!" I smack her on the top of her head. "I mean, do you want me to have a little talk with her and explain the rules about name calling?" I smack my fist into my hand a few times trying to make the point, and her eyes grow about three sizes.

"Oh! No! It's fine. You don't need to go anywhere near her. It's just that she's always kind of hated me, ever since grade three. Not sure why, but I'm used to it by now. She started the whole 'fostergirl' thing. She's just kind of generally mean, but popular at the same time which always amazes me because you would think that being nice would make you popular, wouldn't you, but I'm nice and I'm the furthest thing from popular. I am nice, you know, even though you keep thinking I'm trying to be mean or something to you."

"I know you're nice. What's up with this Eddy guy? I don't think I know who he is. He too stupid to know you're nice?"

"Guys don't want nice. They want beautiful and cutesy and sexy and all kinds of things that I'm not."

"Really." It's been my experience that guys just want girls. I've never had much use for them. Any guys who have pretended to like me were just interested in the fact that I grew a couple of boobs when I was twelve. I mostly hide them under my shirts, but I guess guys have big imaginations.

"Really. I don't know if I'll ever have a boyfriend. Maybe some computer nerd who can't find anyone better."

"I wouldn't worry about it. Guys are mostly not worth the effort."

"I think Eddy is." She sighs and looks off into the distance as if she sees something wonderful, like summer vacation.

"Yeah? Well, if he doesn't like you, I guess he isn't worth much." Her eyes come back and look at me. She looks really surprised. What did I say?

"Wow, Sadie. That's the nicest thing you've ever said to me! You're such a nice person!"

A nice person? That is definitely something I have never

been accused of before. I am absolutely losing my edge. I'm going to have to sharpen up a bit or I'll disappear into lala land with Rhiannon and start seeing rainbows and lollipops everywhere I look.

chapter 23

"I'd like you to look at each of the following pictures carefully and tell me what is missing from each picture."

What's missing from this picture? My mind, that's what. I can't believe I'm here with this dweeby-looking guy listening to him tell me how wonderful it is that I'm letting him do his job. Man, he looks like some kind of accountant or something, all dressed up with a tie wrapped around his pencil neck. He's so formal and uptight I have an urge to grab that tie and give it a good pull, just to see if it would loosen him up a bit. He's so different from Jackson, who is so happy I'm doing this that she's practically dancing around her office. I guess she'd be pretty disappointed if I pulled this guy's tie and snapped his neck.

I am not sure how I got from half-agreeing to talk to Ms. K to all of a sudden sitting here. Well, not so all of a sudden. It's been a couple of weeks or so. I talked to Ms. K the same night I brought the forms home. She didn't really pressure me at all to do it. She just said that I had the right to make up my own mind, but that, if it was her, she would want to know. I'm not her, and I'm not sure I want to know anything about how this guy thinks my brain works, but I decided it was easier to just give in to Jackson because I figured she'd keep on bugging me and getting all the adults in my life involved until I did. Cecilia rushed right over to sign on the dotted line when Ms. K called her. You would think she'd have better things to do, but I guess not. Slow day.

And that's that. Jackson said that we had a super short wait because of my "situation." Meaning that I disappear on a regular basis from every school I've ever been in, I guess. The Kerrys told me I can live there as long as I need to, so I can stay in this school and everything, but there are no guarantees. I don't come with one. I have a habit of messing up everywhere I go and making people who say they want to keep me change their minds and trade me in for a newer model. I come with an unlimited exchange policy.

So here I am, Day Two of wasting everyone's time trying to answer weird questions and make weird block pictures and storyboards and decode bizarre symbols and generally make a fool out of myself in front of Pencilneck. I can't remember his actual name. He's some kind of psychobabble guy from the Board Office or something. Two days of testing, and he'll unlock the secrets of my personal universe. Yeah, right.

"There's no ear on the left side of his head." Picture dude must have been listening to church music.

Pencilneck nods and holds out the next card. He's not very chatty, this guy. I should introduce him to Rhiannon. She'd fill in all his blanks.

"There's no little thingie inside the light bulb."

This is ridiculous. What do light bulbs and earless people have to do with my brain?

"All right, Sadie. We're done. I appreciate the time."

"No prob."

"I'll be back in a couple of weeks with my report. Your parents will be invited to the meeting, and of course you are free to attend if you wish."

I'm free to attend? Is he kidding me? They're talking about my brain here. Of course I don't wish to attend. But I am sure as hell not letting them talk about me behind my back!

"I'll attend. My parents won't because I don't know who they are." I smile sweetly. The face on top of the pencil neck turns into a red eraser.

"Well, your guardian or whoever you live with can attend. Ms. Jackson will figure that out." He packs up all his little easel books and toys into his bag and stands up. He looks kind of uncomfortable, like I'm making him nervous or something. I like adults who I can make feel nervous. You've got to wonder what he's doing testing kids all day if they make him nervous, though. Maybe he needs some psychobabble help of his own.

"So, how did it go?" Jackson pops into the room about a second after Pencilneck scuttles out.

"No idea. None of it really makes any sense or means anything to me."

"That's fair. It wasn't too awful, though, was it?"

"I guess not totally terrible. It wasn't the most fun I've ever had, either."

"I don't imagine it would be."

"He said there would be a meeting or something in a couple of weeks."

"A couple of weeks would be pretty quick but, yes, there will be a meeting at some point."

"He said my parents should come, which is not too likely. Then he said my guardian should come, which is Cecilia."

"Yes."

"Well, does it have to be her?"

"I'm pretty sure it has to be your legal guardian. Why?"

"Oh, nothing. It's OK."

"No, Sadie, it's all right. Tell me what you're thinking."

What am I thinking? Just stupid stuff. Nothing worth saying out loud.

"I was thinking, maybe, Ms. K?" Now, why did I do that? Words coming out of my mouth that should be sitting way down in my throat. I don't even know why I'm thinking it. I mean, she isn't my guardian. She's just another pseudomom who has her own kid to worry about and doesn't have time to come to some stupid meeting for some kid who's only been in her house for a few weeks.

"Of course Ms. Kerry would come. Cecilia and your foster mom can both be here."

"OK. Anyway, I gotta go. See ya." This conversation has gone far enough. I can't trust my mouth, and I never trust Jackson not to say something sappy.

"OK, Sadie. I'm really glad you did this. I'm proud of you." And there it is. Almost got out before she managed it, but not quite quick enough.

Can't handle all these sappy people sometimes. Jackson always talking about how smart I am and what a good student I'm turning into. Rhiannon always telling me how nice I am and what a great friend slash roommate slash fostersister I am. Ms. K talking to me and asking me about my day and listening to my answers like they mean something. It's like I'm trapped in some kind of surreal, parallel universe where Sadie is someone people give a crap about.

I have no idea how to be this Sadie.

"Hi! How'd it go? You were in there so long I thought I might have to come in and rescue you but I couldn't have even if I had tried because Jackson was hovering around the whole time you were there, did you know that? She really likes you, which is kind of cool because she's a really good teacher and everything. I wonder why she was hovering; maybe she thought you'd make a run for it. I kind of thought you might because you hated it so much yesterday and I wondered if you would make it through today. Are we on setting or clearing tonight?"

"Um, I think we're setting and Chandra and Adam are clearing."

"Cool. Let's go home."

Rhiannon heads off down the hall, bopping along like she's dancing, except she has no music. She's one of the only people I know who doesn't always have her MP3 player plugged into her head. I think she has so much going on inside her that any other sounds would just get drowned out by her own babbling brain.

We walk home together most nights. I know hanging out with Rhiannon again makes me one of the totally uncool here, but I pretty much blew the cool thing the minute I walked into the sped room anyway. It doesn't matter. I've never worried about cool. I just make sure everyone understands that I'm not someone they can mess with. No one has really messed with me much at this school so far. I get stared at, and I see the some of the airheads

with too much makeup on whisper to each other about me sometimes, but no one says much out loud. Which is good because it
means I haven't had to smack anyone around yet. Keeps Cecilia
happy and gets me closer to freedom.

"Hey."

The voice is a little familiar, and I stop to see who's actually
talking to me. Rhiannon is still ahead of me, but has stopped and
is waiting at the front door of the school.

"Hi." I don't know her name, but I recognize her from the
group that hangs out by the dumpster. I don't think I've seen her
at all since the second time I tried hanging out there, which isn't
any great loss.

"So, you still go here."

"Guess so."

"Haven't seen you outside much."

"Nope." She makes it sound like I'm missing out.

"Tom asks about you. He thought you were cute or whatever."
She laughs and then starts coughing.

"I have no idea who Tom is and I don't actually care what he
thinks."

"Tom is one of my guys. You met him. He's cool. Except he's
mine. The other guys are relatively cool, too, but I get a little tired
of them sometimes. Could use another girl around to keep them
busy."

"Not interested."

"Whatever. You'd rather hang out with that foster girl kid.
She's a total loser, you know. Makes you look like one, too."

"Your opinion."

"Not just mine. You haven't been here that long. You can still
change things for yourself. You know how it is. I can tell."

"You can tell? You met me twice. You know nothing."

"I know you're screwing yourself at this school."

"Gee, I'm so scared."

"Hey, I'm just trying to help. School sucks enough without the hassles."

"No one hassles me."

"Yet."

"No one hassles me. Ever."

"Yeah, well, I wouldn't bet on it." She starts hacking away again and walks off, probably toward the dumpsters where all the cool kids hang out.

"What did she want?" Rhiannon asks me when I catch up to her at the door.

"Nothing."

"Do you know who she is?"

"Some kid who smokes too much."

"That's not all she does. Her name's Grace Miller. I told you about her, remember? I've known her since I was about five. She's two years older than us. She's been drinking and smoking since like grade seven. There's rumors she's into drugs, too, but I don't know about that. She skips school all the time and hangs out with Tom Shorten and his friends." She says his name like I should know who he is. I look at her and shrug my shoulders.

"Tom Shorten? You never noticed him? Really tall and totally good looking but a real jerk. He hangs out with Grace and a bunch of guys who just like to act tough and make everyone's life miserable. He thinks he's some kind of movie star or something just because his face turned out like a Greek god's and he's all tall and strong and everything and all the girls think he's gorgeous. He's a total player and doesn't care about anyone."

"Never noticed him."

"You must be blind, then. Every girl in school notices him and kind of hopes he'll notice her back. Except me, because I only notice Eddy, who doesn't notice me at all."

"Then Eddy must just be stupid. You want me to talk to him?" I'm really hoping she says no because I don't really have any intention of talking to Eddy or anyone else in the sped room.

"No way! I would absolutely die if you ever talked to him about me! Totally completely and utterly die right in front of you!"

"OK, then I'll keep my mouth shut."

"Thanks Sadie, you're such a good friend. And so nice and understanding and always there for me and…"

I stop the sappy stuff with a handful of leaves which I shove down the back of her shirt. She starts laughing and throwing leaves at me. I start throwing them back, and all of a sudden we're in a total leaf fight on someone's front lawn like two little kindergarten kids getting in trouble at recess. There are leaves in my hair, down my shirt, in my mouth, and a couple stuck up my nose. I can't breathe and my back itches.

I should be pissed, but all I can do is laugh.

chapter 24

"I will do my best to be there."

"OK. Good. Um, thanks. I know it's kind of a pain or whatever." Ms. K looks up from the note in her hand and kind of raises her eyebrows at me.

"It's not a pain. I go to school meetings for all of my kids."

"Well, I haven't been here very long, and I know you have lots to do and…"

"Sadie. I told you when you moved in here that I make a commitment to everyone who comes through that door. As long as you want and need to live here you have a home." She says it straight without any mush attached. It's how she says most things.

"Yeah. I know." I don't look at her when she talks about this stuff. The words make me uncomfortable. She sounds like she believes them, but she doesn't really know me very well.

"Well, actually, I don't think you really know. Yet. You hear my words, but I realize you don't actually believe me."

"I don't think you're a liar!" I don't want to tick her off. Still haven't seen her get really mad, but you have to watch out for the calm ones.

"No, I know you don't think that. But I know you've lived the kind of life that makes it hard to trust people. You're not very old to have had so much to deal with." She doesn't say it like she's feeling all sorry for poor little me. There's no exclamation point at the end, just a period.

"I'm old enough."

"Fifteen going on forty. I know. Anyway, barring any sort of major disaster, I am happy to come to your meeting."

Glad she's happy about it. I'm not happy to go to my own meeting. Pencilneck got his little report done in record time, it seems, and I have to sit down with Cecilia, Jackson, and Ms. K tomorrow to find out that my brain is broken. I wish I had never agreed to all of this in the first place.

"Don't worry about it, Sadie. It will be fine. I wish they would let me go because I know I would make you feel better but students aren't allowed to sit in on another student's parent-teacher interviews and even though this isn't technically a parent-teacher interview it is kind of like one because they will be talking about school stuff and your progress or whatever but you shouldn't worry because I know they'll say you're smart and my mom will be there and she's pretty cool and calm all the time and will make you feel more comfortable and even though you haven't know her really long you still live with her and she is still there on your side. Not that there's sides because everyone is on your side because everyone is there to help you and everything but sometimes it's nice to have someone from your own home on your side. There

I said side again even though I said there aren't any sides. Am I helping?"

"What, sorry? I think I fell asleep. Is it morning?"

"Ha ha. As if I could talk all night long. Although I probably could. We did this exercise in drama class once where the teacher gives you a topic and you have to try to talk for one minute straight on that one topic without pausing and everyone found it really hard to do but me and I talked for like ten minutes on the topic of chalk, which is hard to do because what can you really say about chalk?"

"Knowing you, lots."

"Well, chalk does have lots of uses, you know. Want me to tell you some of them?"

"No, but thanks for the offer. I would like to go to sleep now so that I can stop thinking about the stupid meeting tomorrow."

"No problemo."

"Problemo?"

"I think it's Spanish. Good night, Sadie."

"Good night, Rhiannon."

When Rhiannon decides to go to sleep, it's like turning a switch off on some kind of remote-controlled doll. Her mouth just stops, and she totally winds down in a second. I can hear her breathing over there, already off in dreamland buying ice cream and candy floss.

Wish my brain would turn off. Figures that when I need it to work, like at school, it takes a total holiday, but when I need it to give me a break, it decides to kick into high gear.

The house is so quiet at night. At least this late it is. In the early evening there's so much noise you'd think the neighbors would call the cops. The superbrats aren't too happy with going to bed most nights, and they find a hundred reasons that they aren't quite ready to hit the sack. I want a glass of water. Read me another book. I'm hungry. I'm cold. I want my teddy bear. Sometimes one of them, I think Marie, has a full-out hissy fit. Kicking and screaming and the whole nine yards. Rhiannon told me that the kid had it rough before coming here, which sucks for her, because she's pretty tiny to have already had a tough time. Guess her biomom was a freak and beat on her even though she was an itty bitty kid. Even worse, her biomom's loser boyfriend got in on the act and almost killed her before someone called the cops and got her out of there. I guess I feel sorry for her and all, but I still wish she wasn't so loud about it. Sometimes, she screams in the middle of the night, and I hear Ms. K run into her room to calm her down.

Tonight it's quiet. The inside of my head is the only noisy place. I'm thinking about stuff I don't want to think about. I hate that, when my mind goes places without my permission. I don't want to think about this stupid meeting tomorrow. I don't want to imagine all of their faces when Pencilneck explains to them that I'm brain damaged, and that I'm going to be stupid for the rest of my life. I close my eyes and wait for sleep to come.

"I always suspected that was the case. She has never done well in school." Cecilia sits back and nods. Jackson nods also.

"I kind of suspected it, too. I mean, I never told you, Sadie, because, after all, I've never believed there are stupid kids. Until now. You are definitely stupid."

"Definitely. The tests don't lie. You have a stupid quotient of three million." Pencilneck checks his notes and looks up at everyone with a smile. He's smoking a cigarette and makes an impressive ring that circles everyone's heads. They all applaud.

"Three million what?" I ask, trying not to cough as the smoke flies up my nose.

"Poor thing, see how stupid she is? She doesn't even understand what we're saying." Ms. K pats me on the knee. Pencilneck blows another smoke ring and everyone claps.

"But I thought these tests were supposed to help me!"

"Help you? There is no help for you. You are never going to do anything with your life. Stupid people do not get emancipated." Cecilia shakes her finger at me.

"No help for you, fostergirl!" Why's Rhiannon here? I thought students couldn't come.

"No help for you, fostergirl!" Grace, too? Did they invite the whole school?

"To infinity and beyond, fostergirl!" Buzz Lightyear? Is my brother here, too?

"This meeting is adjourned. Meet you all at the dumpster!" Pencilneck hands out cigarettes to everyone and skips out of the room.

I open my eyes and stare up at the ceiling. Rhiannon is still fast asleep, snoring slightly and totally oblivious. Must be nice.

What good are dreams if they can't shut your brain up for a few hours?

I guess I managed to get back to sleep because all of a sudden it's morning. Rhiannon's already awake and staring at me.

"You OK?"

"Sure. Fine."

"It will be fine. Trust me."

"Sure, I'll trust you, but, unfortunately, I don't think this is up to you." I crawl out of bed and get myself organized to be humiliated.

The meeting isn't until second period, which means I am even spacier than usual during English class. Wilson doesn't even notice. Figures. The class ends faster than usual, which also figures. I stand out in the hall for a second, thinking about maybe spending second period with Grace at the dumpster. Anything would be better than sitting in a room full of adults dissecting my life in front of me. Then I see Ms. K coming down the hall toward me. She gives me her trademark smile, the one that makes you feel like she's in control and you don't have to worry, and for a second I feel a bit better. That is until we walk into Jackson's office and I see Pencilneck sitting there with his papers in front of him that prove what everyone already knows. At least he's not smoking. Maybe that comes later. Cecilia is already there. She smiles at me, too, but it doesn't make me feel like Ms. K's smile does. Jackson is also there and also smiling. Isn't it nice that everyone is so happy?

"So, we are all here to talk about you, Sadie. I have the results from your testing. First I'm going to explain a bit about the tests I conducted, and then I'll share the results. All right with everyone?" They all nod like a bunch of puppets. I don't nod, but he starts talking anyway. I'm not really listening. He's telling them about all the stuff we did and what it means. I know I should listen, but my ears have a kind of roaring sound in them that's making it hard to hear him.

"So, it's kind of like wiring that gets crossed. The thoughts are there but they get a little lost in translation." Wiring? What's he talking about? Is this about the lightbulb again?

"Sadie? Is this making sense to you?" Jackson leans over the table.

"No." Of course not. 'Cause I'm stupid.

"It sounds like a lot of mumbo jumbo. To everyone, not just

you. I'll try to be clearer." Pencilneck, who was introduced to everyone as Steven, looks at me and smiles. Next person who smiles at me is going to regret it. Seriously.

"Everyone has their own way of learning, and some students have more trouble than others. There are many different reasons for this. In your case, the reason seems to be a learning disability."

"Doesn't sound great."

"I guess not. But it's not terrible, either. What it means basically is that you are an intelligent young lady. Your ability to think and reason is considerably above average. But your ability to interpret things you see is below average."

"I can see just fine." I say this just to be obnoxious. Jackson already explained this to me more than once.

"You can see. The images go in and then somewhere along the way to your brain they get a little scrambled. This makes it difficult for you to read at the same level you think. It also makes it difficult to get your thoughts back down onto paper."

"It's like I've been telling you, Sadie. You're a smart girl. You just need a little support so that you can really reach your potential at school." Jackson looks all proud. Of herself or me?

"I would recommend formal identification as learning disabled. This will help her with postsecondary options as well. I've made specific program recommendations here, most of which you have already put in place."

Blah, blah, blah. They keep on babbling and signing papers. I stop listening again, which is kind of interesting when you think of it, because according to Pencilneck listening is the one thing I *can* do.

Everyone seems pleased that I am disabled.

How nice for them.

chapter 25

"Do you want to look at this?" Ms. K is standing at the door of my room with Pencilneck's report in her hand. I don't really want to look at it. For starters, I won't be able to read it, because I have a reading disability or whatever label it was they decided to stamp on my forehead. For finishers, I don't want to.

"Not really,"

"This is good information, Sadie, even though it's telling us something we already knew. You're a smart kid."

"Smart so long as you don't ask me to read or write. Or probably a million other things."

"Not a million other things, but a few. Everyone has things that challenge them. I was never strong in math. Numbers have always been a bit of a mystery to me. I'm not like you. You can problem solve in your head. You've been a great help to Chandra with her math."

"Not so much help." Not sure how I got roped into helping

Chandra in the first place. I'm not much into helping people.
Around here, though, everyone is expected to "pitch in," as Mr. K
calls it. Like a baseball game with Ms. K as the umpire.

"You're wrong about that. She passed that algebra test because
of you."

"Guess I'm just a genius."

"You are very intelligent. We didn't need this report to tell us
that, but it's nice to have it anyway."

"It says I'm disabled. Maybe I should go to school with Adam."
The minute the words spew out I want them back. I seem to be
doing that a lot these days. I don't mean to disrespect Adam. He's
a totally cool person. Ms. K's eyes tell me she's not too impressed.

"Adam has pretty significant needs, Sadie. He has learning
and social issues that make regular school pretty tough for him."
Her voice isn't any more impressed than her eyes.

"Social issues? He seems pretty friendly to me."

"He is very friendly here where he feels safe. Out in the real
world, he has a lot more trouble. He doesn't understand the social
rules people have, and he gets frightened in group situations."

"I have trouble with rules, too." Just other people's rules. Not
my own.

"Lots of people do. It's not the same, though. You know what
they are. You just aren't so sure you want to follow them. But for
Adam, it's a matter of actually not understanding what those rules
are. Simple things like how to start a conversation or even the right
way to walk into a room full of people and let them know he's there.
It's all a learning curve for him, and his school helps him."

"He's not there all day, though, is he?" I'm ignoring her dig
about me not wanting to follow the rules. It's true, of course, but
she isn't supposed to know that or comment on it. Not going to

challenge her, though. She's talking so much about Adam that I think she kind of forgot that she was annoyed with me.

"No. He's integrated for half the day into regular classes where he gets some extra help. It gives him the best of both worlds. How is it that we've migrated from talking about you to talking about Adam? Pretty clever slide there."

"I heard a rumor that I'm pretty clever. Ha ha." She looks at me with a kind of half-smile and shakes her head. She opens her mouth to answer, but Rhiannon comes hopping into the room with her mouth already moving full speed.

"Well, I think you're clever, and I'm sure that report says that you're smart even though I don't know what it says because Mom wouldn't tell me. Not that I asked her, because I knew she wouldn't tell me, because I knew she would say that it is your personal business and if you wanted me to know you would tell me. Do you want me to know?"

"Rhiannon also has trouble sometimes understanding the proper way to walk into a room full of people and start a conversation," Ms. K says, gently smacking Rhiannon on the top of the head. Rhiannon laughs and rubs her head like it hurts. Ms. K ruffles her hair and Rhiannon pushes her away, still laughing.

"You can read it if you want. It's all, what did Pencilneck call it? Oh, mumbo jumbo."

"Pencil neck?" Ms. K sounds confused.

"Yeah, didn't you notice his neck? All stiff and skinny and looking like it would snap if you pushed on it." Ms. K tries to look all disapproving for a second, but then she laughs at me. For a second she looks like she might try to ruffle my hair, too, but she doesn't. For a piece of a second I kind of wish she had. A little tiny piece.

"Come to think of it, he did look a little uptight. Maybe he was intimidated by all of the beautiful and intelligent women in the room."

"Yeah, right. Anyway. You can tell Rhiannon about the report or meeting or whatever. It's no secret. I'm already a sped. According to this thing, I'm in the right place."

"What I heard is that, according to this *thing*, you're an intelligent young woman with a few learning challenges that you can learn to overcome. You're already doing it with Ms. Jackson. If you gave yourself a break here for even a second, you'd let yourself look at how far you've come in just a few short months." Ms. K's face is all serious now. She's still holding the report out in my direction, and I still don't want to take it. I mean, I always knew I had trouble in reading, but I always figured if I really started to try to do better, I would be able to do it. I never figured I had some wiring problem on top of all my other messed up problems that would sentence me to life as a reading reject.

"It's just like with Eddy. He's totally smart in class when we're having discussions and things and he's always got the answers when he's talking. His oral reports are totally amazing, but he has all kinds of problems when he tries to write down the stuff he knows, so the teachers sometimes let him do his tests out loud at the back and the people in the back rows try to listen except he talks too quietly. He uses the computer, too, and sometimes does his tests and stuff in the spe…I mean, resource room."

"You seem to know an awful lot about this Eddy person. Is there something I should know?" Ms. K finally puts the report down and turns her attention to Rhiannon. I breathe a sigh of relief. I don't like to be center stage. Not used to someone pushing so hard to make me feel good about things that don't seem particularly good to me. Except for Jackson, that is. She never gives up, and I know she'll be ragging on me about this report the minute I walk into school.

"No, Mother. Just a boy." Rhiannon closes her mouth firmly, which of course is a dead giveaway to her mom. That, and the fact that her face has turned the color of a hot chili pepper.

"Oh, I see. Well, I hope he is just a nice boy and recognizes quality when he sees it."

"Mom!" Rhiannon turns even redder and walks out of the room. Ms. K grins at me, and I find myself grinning back. Maybe I should talk to this Eddy kid for Rhiannon. I mean, maybe he just doesn't know she likes him. Maybe he would like her back. Then again, maybe he would pretend to like her, get her to spend time with him doing things she doesn't really want to do, and then dump her and tell everyone at school she's easy. I can feel my grin disappear.

"I think I'll go talk to her," I tell Ms. K, who looks pleased. I feel a little guilty because I'm not really going to talk to her. I have no idea what to say to her about boys in general and I'm not ready to make any offers about this Eddy kid until I know more about him. There's a chance he's OK. Not sure how I'll figure that out, but I guess I could try. Somehow.

Right now I have to think about other stuff. My birthday is coming up, and I'll be sixteen. I checked, and the agency hasn't changed the emancipation age…yet. If they haven't done it by now, I figure they won't have it done by my birthday, and I won't be stuck with the whole changing-it-to-eighteen thing. Man, first the school system and now the foster system. It's like the whole world wants to keep us as little kids until we're eighteen. Who's to say that eighteen is better than sixteen? I know kids who are totally immature at eighteen and I know other kids who are totally ready to be on their own at fifteen…like me, for example. I'm more mature than half the kids in grade twelve right now. I still have to try to persuade Cecilia to try to persuade the board that I'm ready to fly on my own.

She's as stiff as Pencilneck, though, and I haven't figured out how to loosen her up. She seemed pretty happy about the report and all. Maybe I should pretend that I'm happy about it, too, and that I believe all that crap about being smart enough for college and that I'll go there if she lets me live on my own. I have to figure out how to persuade her that I can work and go to school at the same time, both in high school and later in my imaginary college. I know I could because I don't do homework anyway, so I could work every day from like three until ten or something and make lots of money. But I'm pretty sure she would think that I should devote all my time to studying. As if. Maybe if I can find a job that will let me work those hours and then tell her I have it, she'll be so impressed that she'll cut me loose. Maybe.

Maybe she'd also be impressed if I ask her to let me in on my family secrets. She keeps saying I'm old enough to know about my own past if I want to and that she has some kind of information for me. Pretty sure it isn't going to be information that brightens up my day or anything. Can't think of something wonderful she can say that would explain why I don't live with my own family. If I have one. But maybe if I suck it up and make myself listen to her, she'll think I'm all mature and able to handle life. Life on my own, that is.

Ms. K keeps telling me I can stay with them until I'm ready to go. She doesn't mean two months, either. She means until the end of high school. She thinks she can put up with me for two and a half more years, which might be a record for me in one house. What she doesn't know yet is that I have a special talent.

I can make anyone regret their decision to take me in and then find a reason to send me packing. I don't even have to try. It just comes naturally to me. So talented.

I wonder what it would be like to live here until I'm an actual society-approved adult. To be part of this weird family and to listen to Rhiannon talk for the next two years.

It would probably drive me nuts. I mean, they're nice and all, but they're always in my face. Everyone in my business and either giving me some kind of chore to do or telling me how much potential I have. I'd rather do the chores than listen to the cheer-leading squad singing "go Sadie go." It's all so sucky and sweet. A person can only take so much of it.

Besides, they really don't know me yet. I might have a lot of potential, but it's not the kind that they're thinking about.

chapter 26

"You have a good placement with the Kerrys. I'm sorry, Sadie, but I still see no reason to recommend early release from foster care for you."

"That's not fair! You know I've wanted this forever! I can find a job. I talked to a couple of places last week, and they told me to come back when I'm sixteen. I can take care of myself! You can supervise me or whatever, check in. I don't mind. Just let me get a place!" I sound like I'm begging, which isn't cool. I have to calm down so she'll listen to me.

"Sadie, the Board very seldom recommends early release from care. It is only in extreme cases, and most often for someone for whom we can't find a better situation. You have a better situation. You can stay with the Kerrys until you're eighteen and then just walk away if you want. But you can stay with them longer if you want to go on in school."

"I don't even want to stay in school now. It sucks and I suck

191

at it." I did it again. I didn't mean to say that. I meant to say that I agree with her and that I want to go on in school. I meant to lie and instead I told the truth. What's the matter with me?

"But the report says…"

"I don't want to talk about the stupid report. It says that school sucks and I suck at it. Period."

"It says you're smart."

"Yeah, yeah. So I hear. Well, if I'm so smart you should let me live on my own before they change the rules and I can't."

"I thought you liked the Kerrys."

"I like them fine. It's not about that! It's not like they're my real family or anything. I don't have one of those, remember? There's just me, and I want it to be just me."

"This might be the time to talk about your real family."

I open my mouth to tell her I don't want to hear it, and then I close it again. I already screwed up on the school angle. She's sitting there handing me the chance to try Plan B. I still don't really want to hear it, but I guess I have to try anything.

"OK."

"OK?" She looks confused. Which is the way she usually looks around me. Guess she was expecting my usual answer.

"OK, go ahead. Tell me all the wonderful things about my real family." I feel like I want to cover my ears, but that would look stupid. Besides, who cares anyway? Nothing she says can bother me. It's a story about strangers. Just like a TV movie. It doesn't really have anything to do with me. Not really.

"All right. You're sure you want to do this right now? You aren't in a great frame of mind."

"My mind is framed just fine. It's my history. You have to give it to me. You told me that enough times."

"All right then. I think you already know bits and pieces."

"Yeah, like the whole door-to-door begging routine. That true?" I'm looking away from her. I need that blank wall from Jackson's room to stare at.

"Yes, unfortunately. Your mother was on her own with the two of you children, and she was having some pretty serious substance abuse problems. At one point she left you alone for a few days. Your brother managed to feed the two of you from the food in the house, but when that ran out he took you to the neighbors' to ask for food. They alerted the police, who then alerted us and you went into care."

I'm still looking at my imaginary blank wall. The story of my life in a hundred words or less. Nothing new to my ears except the druggy part. I guess drugs are more interesting than kids to some people.

"How old was she?"

"Your mother? In her early twenties, I believe. She had been married to your father but he left soon after you were born and was never heard from again as far as I know."

Early twenties. Old enough to know better. Not some teenager who didn't know how to control her life. A grownup. Man, I quit smoking when I was fourteen.

"How old was I?" Not that it matters much.

"You were three and your brother Christopher was almost five."

Christopher. Chris. I had that part right. Maybe my brain doesn't have as many holes in it as I thought.

"And she left us alone." Don't know why I'm saying it again. Sounded bad enough when Cecilia said it.

"Yes. Sometimes people lose control of their lives and priorities, and children get caught in the middle. I'm sorry that this happened to you."

"You didn't do it. You don't need to be sorry." My mother's the one who should apologize.

"Anyway, your mother is now living in a city a couple of hours' drive from here and is holding down a job."

"How nice for her." Why would I care? She's not part of my life. This is why I didn't want to hear all of this crap in the first place. I just don't care. This better be worth it. Cecilia better be impressed by my maturity here, because I am not enjoying this.

"There is a chance that you could reconnect with her at some point. When you're ready. She has approached the agency and indicated that she would be interested in seeing you."

I wasn't expecting that. I don't have an answer so I just stay quiet.

"Your brother also would like to see you again." I turn to look at her. My brother. Chris. Do I remember him? Can I remember him feeding me and taking me out so other people could feed me?

"Where is he?" Not that I would know him. He wouldn't feel like my brother. Just another guy.

Cecilia doesn't answer at first. She looks uncomfortable, like she's wishing that the conversation was already over. I stare at her until she's forced to answer.

"Actually, he still lives with your mother."

"What?" I don't think I heard her right. He can't be in the system and live with my mother at the same time. We were both taken away. Right?

Cecilia kind of sighs and looks like she wishes she hadn't ever opened her mouth.

"Your mother worked hard to go straight after you two were

taken away. A couple of years after you went into the system, she made an appeal to the court to have your brother returned to her custody. She was successful and he has lived with her ever since. Sadie, I know this is hard to hear and I wish I could tell you something different, but I owe you the truth. It was nothing to do with you personally. She just felt overwhelmed at the thought of trying to raise two children on her own and decided you would be better off with someone different raising you."

I'm still staring at her. My ears are working, but obviously I can't process words anymore because nothing she is saying is making any sense to me. My mother took my brother back and not me? He grew up in a house with a mother while I got bounced around from house to house like a rejected tennis ball?

"Someone different? Twelve foster parents or whatever it is now?"

"In fairness to her, Sadie, she thought you would be adopted by a nice family. It just didn't turn out that way." She reaches out to touch me. I slap her hand away. I don't care if that counts as violence and she calls my PO. I want to slap her in the mouth hard enough to bury all of her stupid words back inside her pathetic brain where they belong.

"Fairness? You have to be kidding me. There's nothing fair here. My brother lives with his mommy, and I'm in another stupid foster home with people who don't want me."

"The Kerrys do want you," she says, as if that's the point. Which it isn't. She's also wimping out and changing the subject. Fine with me. I'm done talking about my so-called real family. I don't want to know anything else about them. Ever.

"I've been in enough houses to know the score with this place. They're not the first people to say they want to make nice and keep me for a while. It never actually happens, and I don't even want it to."

"The Kerrys are different."

"You said that about the Thompsons. I even changed my last name when I lived with them. Mrs. Thompson told me to call her Mom. I don't see them anywhere, do you?" That shut her up. Cecilia just looks at me like she's trying to come up with some lie that won't make her look like a liar.

"Don't worry about it, C, I know you don't have a snappy comeback for that one. I know how it is. I've been around awhile. You can tell me all the wonderful crap in the world and that won't make it true. I can only trust me, and I only want to live with me. Why can't you get that?"

"I do understand. But I don't think it's in your best interest right now."

"What if I find a job and prove to you I can work and do school at the same time? Then will you think about it?" She looks at me for a minute and I can tell by her eyes that she's giving up the argument. Probably feels guilty that she just told me my mother and brother lived happily ever after without me. Fine. I'll use that if it gets her to reconsider.

"I will think about it, I guess. But don't get your hopes up. I can't promise anything, and I don't know if or when the age limit is going to change."

"Don't worry about me. I never get my hopes up."

Why would I? It's just like Buffy told me. You let yourself think something good is going to happen, and then you go flying up with your hopes just so you can come down harder when everything crashes. It's easier to expect the worst. Most of the time, the worst happens anyway, so you might as well be ready for it. I expected the worst when I finally let Cecilia tell me about my life and I got slammed to the ground with it anyway. Imagine how I'd be feeling now if I'd expected good news.

I wonder for just a second how Alisha is doing with her aunt. I wonder if she still has hope.

Right now, my hope is buried so far underground that I would need a shovel to dig it up.

chapter 27

Cecilia leaves and I head over to the school. She came first thing in the morning so I wouldn't miss much school, but I've already missed first period and, if I walk slowly enough, I might manage to miss second period, too. Of course, the school is only a ten-minute walk away so I only manage to slow it down enough to arrive in time for the second half of the period. I stand on the edge of the school lawn, thinking about walking backwards and starting over again.

I let myself think about what Cecilia said about my so-called family for a second, but then I put it away. It's not worth more than a second of thought. My mother and my brother haven't been more than a stupid dream for the past twelve years. Why should I feel anything about them now? I sure as hell don't want to see either of them just because they woke up one morning and decided they feel guilty about leaving me to the mercy of the system. I'm fine on my own. I do OK. They have their life and I have mine. End of that story.

I see a wisp of smoke from the side of the school. Grace and company. Not very good company, but better than Wilson and easier than walking backwards.

"Hi." Grace looks at me with kind of a "knew you would come back" look. Looking at her little guy gang, I can figure out which one is that Tom guy, standing there looking like he thinks he's god's gift to girls. He looks at me in that player-dude-forgetting-that-the-girl-he's-checking-out-has-a-head kind of way. Makes me want to grab his chin and shove his head up to face level. Except that would mean touching him which would probably make him think I'm interested. It makes me want to wash my hands or something.

"Hi."

"So, had enough of being a model student?" Grace always sounds sarcastic and like she thinks she's better than me. Loser.

"I'm no model student. I've just been trying to keep clean so I can get my own place." Why did I tell her that? It's none of her business. Now I'm acting like a loser.

"Your own place? Your parents are cool with that?" Tom looks impressed. I open my mouth to answer but Grace is faster.

"Foster parents, right? You live with that Rhiannon kid," she says with a smile that doesn't exactly look friendly. What am I doing here?

"Man, that sucks. She's a total freak fest, isn't she?" Tom says. One of his stupid henchmen laughs. I don't.

"She's OK." I should probably say more to defend her, but I don't.

"So, how do you get your own place?" Tom asks, looking actually interested. Grace kind of glares at him. Guess he's not supposed to be interested in anyone but her.

"It's a foster care thing. When I hit sixteen, I can ask to be let go. I get my own apartment and a job and everything. No big deal." Except that it is a big deal and it probably isn't going to happen and I'll have to find another way to get out. And it isn't any of his business and I really need to bite my tongue in half so that I stop talking.

"That would be awesome. Party every night!" Tom looks at me like I'm a cheeseburger and he's starving. I stare him down, but he just kind of grins at me. I can see where other girls might think he has a nice smile. It looks like those smiles you see on movie guys, only this one is on a creepy guy.

"Whatever. I'm not there yet."

"So, does it suck living with the Kerrys? I hear they have all kinds of weird little foster kids living there all the time." Grace moves over so she's standing in front of Tom. She leans back against him and blows smoke in my face.

"Like me, you mean." Might have to tap into my aggressive side and see if she wants to swallow that cigarette.

"No, you don't seem weird. You seem pretty cool to me. Cute, too." Tom turns up the volume on his smile. He thinks it makes him look cuter. He's wrong. Grace seems to agree with me on that one and leans back against him again, only this time I see an elbow go into his gut.

"Yeah, cute is so what I'm going for."

Tom laughs. He gives Grace a little push and steps away from her.

"Well, you're not a freak fest anyway. We've got a party on tonight. You want to come?" Grace glares at him again, but he ignores her. The other guys look at each other and laugh.

"Not much into parties these days." I used to be. I used to

do my share of drinking and other recreational-type activities that would make Cecilia have a heart attack if she knew about all of them. I haven't bothered with that stuff since I moved here, though. Part of my master plan to get out. The only party I've had is Rhiannon style—watching movies and eating ice cream straight from the container. What am I turning into?

"You will be into this one. You need to meet a few new people. You can't spend your whole life at that house with all those little kids. You'll lose your mind."

He has a point. I mean, if no one else is going to try to help me escape my life, why shouldn't I listen to him? All Cecilia managed to do is to make me realize that my whole stupid life sucked even more than I thought it did and that it isn't going to change any time soon. That my own so-called mother decided that I suck so much that she left me with strangers while she hung out with my brother. I need some breathing space here. I'm entitled to a good time, away from the superbrats and Rhiannon's chatter and Ms. K's all-seeing eyes. Away from thinking about things I don't want to think about. Besides, it would be worth it just to piss Grace off completely.

"I might come."

"That's cool. Meet us back here at eight if you're coming."

Tom walks off and the other guys follow him like brainless baby ducks. Grace blows a puff of smoke into my face and waddles off after them. Obviously we are not destined to be best friends. How sad. She doesn't appear to like me. Which appears to be something to do with the fact that I am female and therefore must be interested in Tom. I'd tell her she doesn't need to worry, but it's more fun ticking her off.

I don't know if I'll go or not, but at least I managed to miss the rest of English class. It's lunchtime by the time I actually head up the stairs of the school. I usually go to Jackson's room during lunch, but I think I'll pass on that today. She'll want to talk about the report and college or whatever, and I'm not up for that right now. I'm tired of being told how happy I should be that I'm brain damaged.

I stand in the front hall and watch as all the classroom doors open up and vomit out hungry kids. Maybe I'll try the cafeteria. But if I go there I'll have to sit with Rhiannon and that kid with the braces. I'm not up for that right now, either.

Screw it. I'm not sitting in the cafeteria with the dweeb brigade, and I'm not sitting in the resource room with the sped brigade.

Maybe I should figure out where the dumpster gang hangs out during lunch. Guess they don't actually eat at the dumpster, which is probably a testament to some level of intelligence.

At least none of them cares if I'm smart or not, or if I go to college or not, or finish my homework or not. They don't care if I have a family who wants me or not. They don't even care if I'm nice or not. I'm not sure what they care about except having a good time and not worrying about anything that isn't part of that good time.

Sounds like a fine attitude to me.

chapter 28

"Where are you going?"

"Nowhere important. Just out with a couple of friends."

"Oh. I didn't know you had any friends. No, that didn't come out right. Sorry. Well, you know what I mean, don't you?"

"Yeah, I know you didn't mean anything. It's no big deal. Just a couple of people I met in class. Decided I need to branch out a little."

"Oh. Well, do I know them?"

"Oh, probably. You seem to know everyone. I can't remember their names. You know how I am with names."

"Yeah, you do suck at names. I don't think you even know everyone here yet!" She laughs at me and looks at me with trusting eyes. I feel guilty for a second, but it's really for her own good. After all, Grace was so totally mean to Rhiannon that it's better for her not to know that she's one of the people I'm going to see. I know she'd be all worried and bent out of shape if she knew I was hanging with Grace and Tom. Rhiannon is from a different world, kid-wise, and she thinks kids like Grace are dangerous or something. What Rhiannon has never figured out is that I am a hell of a lot more dangerous than any kid she knows. When I want to be.

"Anyway, did you tell Mom you're going out? She needs to know where everyone is all the time."

"Yeah, I told her." Lie number two. I've always been really good at lying. Someone told me once it's because my eyes are so dark that no one can read what I'm thinking. Not sure if that was a compliment. Probably not. I give Rhiannon what I hope is a reassuring smile and head downstairs. It's just before eight, which I know is the time Ms. K is busy fighting to put the superbrats to bed. Mr. K always helps her, so I know the coast is clear. By the time they finish that, they usually take some quiet time and leave the older kids on our own in our rooms to do homework or whatever. They'll never even notice I'm gone. I hope.

I know it might have been easier to just try the same lie on Ms. K that I did on Rhiannon, but I'm not sure it would work on her. She has this weird, like, ESP thing when it comes to lying. I watch her catch the other kids at it all of the time. She gets really bent out of shape when someone lies. Goes on about trust and honesty and other such garbage. Since neither trust or honesty ranks very high on my list of important things, I decide it's not worth the potential hassle when I can just sneak out and back in without her noticing. I hope.

I get to the dumpster a couple of minutes after eight. Tom and Grace are there with the other guys who still don't have names inside my head. Tom looks happy to see me. Grace does not.

"Let's go then," Tom says as I walk up. Not wasting any time on conversation. That's a nice change. Everyone turns to pile into an old car that looks like the wheels might fall off if we drive too fast. I hesitate for just a second, wondering if I should just head back to the house before Rhiannon accidentally tells Ms. K that I went out. Maybe I should have risked the honesty lecture and just told Ms. K I was going over to a friend's house.

Too late now. I'm not going to worry about it. All I'm doing is trying to find a good time. I earned it. I let Cecilia tell me the big family secret so she could get it off her chest and plaster it onto mine. Now I know that my mother is a bigger loser than I could have even imagined and that I don't need to wonder about my brother any more because he isn't really my brother. He's my mother's son. And I'm just me.

I've been a good little girl at school, and I did the stupid testing and even sat through the meeting from hell. I totally deserve some time off the sunshine-and-roses train. I climb into the back seat and squeeze between the two nameless guys. Grace smiles at me from the front seat, a "see, I'm sitting with Tom and you're not" kind of smile. I smile back an "I don't care what you do" kind of smile.

We take off at top speed, which is probably not all that fast seeing as the car is a reject from the junk yard. The car still feels pretty shaky, and I would tell Tom to slow down except that the guys without names would probably shove me out onto the road if I did and laugh at me as I roll away into the ditch.

We head downtown. Not that this town is really big enough to have an uptown and a downtown, but there's a set of railway tracks that separates the town in half. People always say they live uptown, which is above the tracks, or downtown, which is below. The Kerrys live uptown. The party is obviously downtown. How exciting. I get to see how the other half lives. Ha ha. Funny Sadie.

Not even sure why we're driving because everything in this town is walkable. I don't figure Tom for a Pepsi drinker, either, so his driving is probably kind of dicey. On the other hand, the drive is short. He probably knows his way around town with his eyes shut.

We get to the party in about three minutes. This is a good thing because the nameless guys are also apparently showerless guys. I'm pretty happy to get out and breathe in the semi-fresh air. We're at a house on a dead-end street. It's a pretty small-looking house with an unbelievable number of bodies crammed into it. It looks like one of those world-record things where ten people try to squeeze into an old Volkswagen bug car. I swear there're like a hundred kids squished into a house that's made for a family of three.

Pretty obvious that the family isn't home. No evidence of a parent of any description, which makes sense. Wouldn't be much of a party with a mom or a dad hovering around.

Tom and Grace are already in the house. The nameless guys have disappeared, and I'm standing by myself beside the rusted-out car wondering what I'm doing here. I mean, I know what to do at a party. I've been to lots of them in other places I've lived. It was a party like this that got me kicked out of my last foster home.

It was all so stupid. The other fostergirl in my house and I were totally bored on a Friday night and decided to find something to do. We managed to find a party and headed over at around ten thirty or so. We weren't supposed to be out past eleven, but that never stopped us. We had ways of sneaking out and sneaking back in. Our pseudomom wasn't too bright; or maybe she just didn't care. Never was sure which. Didn't matter.

Everyone at the party was already pretty out of it by the time we got there. We each had a couple of drinks, but we couldn't catch up to everyone else. A little while after we got there, a couple of completely wasted guys decided to start hassling us, getting all gropey and disgusting. One of them grabbed Janey and tried to force her into a bedroom. He was so out of it he probably couldn't have done much to her anyway, but she got scared and started to scream. Her screaming just disappeared into the music so no one heard her but me. No one would have done anything even if they had heard her. No one cared. Except me. I've never had much use for guys in general, and I don't put up with guys who hassle girls. I didn't even think about it. I just grabbed a knife out of the kitchen and used it to let the jerk know he had to make other plans.

I didn't actually stab him, though I would have if he hadn't backed down. Which he did immediately because, like most guys I've met, he was a total coward on top of being a jerkwad. A couple of other kids saw me threaten him and decided to get all panicky and called the cops. Unbelievable. Everyone there was underage and either drunk or stoned, and these babes call the cops! Anyway, I got arrested, even though the guy was trying to rape my friend.

I ended up with probation. First offense. That they knew about. Extenuating circumstances. Whatever. Released to Cecilia who had to make her phone calls to find me a new place because my pseudofamily didn't want trouble in their happy home. Exit Sadie.

Strange to think that Buffy and I actually had something in common after all.

"Hey, aren't you coming in?" Tom has actually come back out of the sardine can to find me. Which would seem nice, but I know he's just trying to play me. That's cool. I can handle players. I just have to find the kitchen.

"Sure. Just wasn't sure where I would fit. Seems a little tight in there." He laughs like I said something brilliantly funny.

"Small house, big crowd. It's all good. Lots to drink inside. You look thirsty. Come on." He leads the way and the crowd kind of parts to let us through. Tom's super tall and kind of big all over, and people notice him when he walks. I just truck along inside his shadow and no one notices me. Story of my life.

"Beer? Rye? What's your pleasure?" He gestures at a table full of bottles.

"How'd they afford all this?"

"Oh, it's a BYOB and then they just throw it all together."

"I didn't bring anything."

"That's cool. No one knows the difference. Help yourself."

Haven't had a drink since I moved here. Been turning into a nun. I mix myself a rye and coke in a plastic cup and sip it. It actually tastes gross, but I drink it anyway. Tom sucks back a beer or two and then drifts off into the mess of bodies so they can worship him close up.

I just kind of stay in a corner and watch. I don't really know anyone and don't really want to. I recognize a face or two. I'm surprised to see the Eddy of Rhiannon's dreams over on the other side of the room. Guess he isn't the one for her after all. I don't think anyone who would fit with Rhiannon would be at a place like this.

Don't know what that says about me.

"This party blows. There's another one back uptown. Let's check it out." Grace and Tom suddenly materialize in front of me. Not sure how they found me. Not sure Grace even wanted to. No one else was paying any attention to me, and I thought I had managed to become invisible again.

I go with them because I don't really have much choice. I still don't know this reject town well enough to find my street after dark. I don't really want to go to another pathetic excuse for a party, but I don't want to give Grace the satisfaction of thinking I'm a loser because I ask to go home. So, we squish ourselves back into the rusted rat trap, which doesn't feel as crowded now after standing in that house, and start to creak our way back across town.

It doesn't take long to head toward the tracks again. Close enough that speed doesn't matter. Probably could have walked, but I guess I'm just lazy. I can hear a train making that obnoxious warning sound that bellows through town about ten times a day. I seem to remember actually kind of liking trains at some point in my life. I think I liked to imagine where they came from and where they were going, back when I still let myself imagine things. I kind of remember liking it when a car I was in had to wait for a train to go by so I could look at the train cars and wonder what was in them and make up stories about the families inside.

I don't make up stories any more. And I don't think I like trains. They make too much noise.

We're heading for the bridge. There's a long way around that takes you under the train instead of in front of it. I wonder what Tom's going to do. We're obviously still heading in the direction of the whistle. He's moving pretty fast, at least as fast as this heap can move. Too fast to turn at the bridge, so he must be staying on the main road.

We're coming up on the crossing and I'm watching for the train. I can see it coming across the bridge and I sit back, waiting for Tom to stop.

"Go for it!" Nameless Guy Number One yells in my ear. What's he talking about?

"Totally!" Tom yells back from the front seat and the car kind of jerks forward, trying to speed itself up.

By the time my brain registers what's about to happen, it's too late. All I can hear is the impossible sound of the train hitting the car as it pushes us down the tracks and down off the bridge in a grinding, screaming mass of tangled-up metal and people. I can hear horrible screams as we actually fall off the bridge onto the road below.

The last thing I remember is realizing that the screams are coming from me.

chapter 29

Murky images flash through my mind like sudden jolts of pain. I hear crying and screaming and see faces that I don't recognize looking down at me and asking me questions that I can't find any answers for. I see darkness. Can darkness really be seen?

Am I in an ambulance? I can hear a siren taking turns with voices of strangers asking me to look at things and asking me if I know my name. Of course I know my name! It's other people's names I don't know. I try to tell them but I can't keep my eyes open, and my mouth won't say what I want it to.

Now I'm at the hospital. How did I get here so fast? How did I get out of the ambulance and into this room? Doctors and nurses running around trying to sound important while they check me over to make sure I'm not broken in places that don't show. I don't feel broken, but my brain's fogged over. What the hell happened? Where is everyone? I want to ask but my mouth is still not working, so my questions stay inside my messed-up mind.

People put their hands on me and I can't seem to stop them. Now I'm in some kind of bed. My head is a little clearer but it still feels like lead and I can't seem to control it enough to turn and look around, so all I can do is listen. My best trick. I hear lots of beeping and some moaning that sounds like a horror movie.

No one is really talking to me, but I know that I've been in an accident, and that I am in horrible trouble. I know I messed up again in a spectacular fashion. I just have to lie here and wait for Cecilia to come and tell me where I'm going next. Stupid Sadie.

I drift in and out of consciousness as people drift in and out of my room. I listen to them talking but can't place the voices. Some of them sound familiar. I even hallucinate that I can hear Rhiannon but I know that can't be. Rhiannon and her family are history now.

"Hi there," a nurse says, looking into my eyes.

"Hi," I think I manage to say.

"You were pretty lucky, you know. You have a concussion and some bruising and that's about it."

I don't feel lucky. I feel stupid. Lucky would have been staying home and watching movies with Rhiannon. Home. Don't have one of those any more. Again.

"The others?"

"Everyone survived."

She's not telling me much. That's OK because I don't really want to know much.

The doctor comes in later and tells me why I got so lucky. That word again. He said they figure that I was the most protected, wedged in between two big guys. I was bruised by the seat belt where I jerked forward against it. I got a concussion because Nameless Guy Number One rammed into me when we landed, and they think his head actually bashed into mine, knocking us both out for a minute or two. My head will likely hurt for days and the bruises are big and sore, but that's all.

He tells me it was some kind of miracle that we didn't all die. Or I guess it was more like a whole bunch of mini-miracles that added up to the big one.

Tom's car got far enough over the tracks that we were hit behind the back passenger door and pushed along the tracks for just a few yards until we were actually forced off the bridge onto the road below. The train was going slowly. The bridge is a low one. No cars were on the road below us. Our town is so small that everyone heard the crash and help arrived almost immediately.

It all adds up to being hit by a train and still being alive.

"Sadie? Are you all right? Can you hear me?" My eyes are closed again and I want to keep them that way. Forever if possible. I want to keep my ears and mouth closed, too. The voice is insistent, though, and I can feel breath on my face. Doesn't sound like the nurse. I open one eye and try to focus on the face, but it's swimming around in front of me and making me nauseous, so I close it again.

"Sadie? Are you OK? Sadie? WAKE UP!" The sheer panic in her voice penetrates my weak brain and I manage to open my eyes for a second.

"Honey, relax, the nurse said she'll be fine. She's just sleeping."

"She usually wakes up when I bother her when she's sleeping though. She isn't now. I knew I should have made her tell me where she was going. I should have followed her or something.

She doesn't know the kids in this town, and she didn't know what she was getting into! It's all my fault." She's crying.

"No , it's not your fault. Sadie's a big girl and she knew what she was doing. I don't know what she was thinking, but it isn't anything to do with you."

"Right," I think I manage to say, but I can't really hear my own voice. My eyes shut again.

"Sadie? You said something. Mom, she talked, I heard her. Sadie?"

"Rhiannon, maybe we should go and let her rest. We'll come by tomorrow."

"But I want to talk to her! She needs me."

"Just come and let her rest. You go wait for me with Cecilia. I'll be right out."

Cecilia. I was expecting her. I was not expecting Rhiannon and her mother, but I'm pretty sure I'm not hallucinating any more.

"Sadie? The nurse said you can probably hear me. You have a concussion. They will have to keep waking you up so you don't fall into a deep sleep. They gave you some pain medication. You have some bad bruising on your chest also." Her voice sounds odd, but then again everything sounds odd to me at the moment. It's quiet for a second and I figure she's gone.

"I can't believe you did this! I can't believe you put yourself in this position. Look at you! You could have been killed!"

"Lily." A soft voice interrupts her. She's almost yelling at me, which is what I expected Cecilia to do. I don't think I've ever heard Ms. K actually yell before. Kind of sucks that our last conversation has to be so loud. But I totally deserve it. Bring it on.

"Brad. Look at her. Did you see the car?"

"I know, Lil. But she's OK. The doctor said she's going to be fine." Mr. K? What's he doing here? Who's at home with the little superbrats?

"What was she thinking, getting into a car with those boys. Going out without telling me. What were you thinking?" She seems to be talking to me.

"I don't think she can answer you right now. We'll deal with it later." Mr. and Ms. K seem to have switched roles. He's all calm and in control, and she's the one who sounds out of whack.

"We most definitely will. There are rules that I expect everyone to follow. Even when they don't want to!" She seems to be talking to me again. Which is weird, because I'm not talking back.

"Lily, this isn't the time or the place. She needs to rest." I can hear them. I don't want to hear them. I want to go to sleep or pass out or whatever you do with a concussion and stop hearing them.

Why did I get in that car? Good question. I don't have an answer at the moment because my head feels unbelievably strange. Not pain but pressure, like someone is pushing down on my forehead with all their strength, trying to shove it to the back of my skull.

"I just don't know what to think, Brad. This is so unlike her. She seems so mature and reasonable."

"Let's just wait until she's feeling better and we'll talk to her. She can tell us what happened."

"All right. Can you go find Rhiannon? She's out there somewhere in the waiting room with Cecilia. She'll be frightened and worried. She'll need you to tell her again that Sadie's OK."

"All right."

Rhiannon's mom stays with me for a second. She doesn't say anything but I can hear her breathing or maybe she's sighing. I can't tell. Then she leans over and it feels like she brushes her lips against my cheek. More hallucinations.

Rhiannon. How had she heard about it? Small town, I guess. She sounded so upset. Did I do that to her?

My head is starting to hurt underneath all the pressure and my brain is starting to shut down. My thoughts are tripping over each other. I need them to stop so I can sleep and disappear from this.

One final thought, though. What did Ms. K mean by rules? What's the point in setting rules for someone who's going away?

chapter 30

"Sadie?"

"Yes?"

"Can you come here for a minute, please?"

"OK, just a second."

"No, right now! It will be too late in a second. We'll miss the train."

"The train! I didn't know we were going on a trip!" I run toward her, excited at the promise of an adventure. She's standing down the street from me, just kind of waiting in the middle of the road.

"Where are we going?" I ask as I try to make my pudgy little legs move me faster down the street so I don't upset her by making us late. I don't like to upset her.

"Oh, we aren't going anywhere. You're going alone."

I catch up to her and she grabs me. She isn't standing in the street at all but on the track the train goes on. It's dark out, which I

217

hadn't noticed before, and it feels cold. I'm shivering, even though she's holding me tightly.

"What do you mean? Where am I going alone?" I feel my stomach start to hurt. I hope I don't throw up on her because that would probably upset her. I tell my stomach to behave itself.

"You'll see," she says, still holding me. I can hear a loud noise coming from far down the tracks. There's a tiny light that's getting bigger and bigger as the train comes closer to us. My stomach is hurting more and more and I start to wiggle around, trying to get her to let go.

"Stop moving. You are upsetting me!" She yells, trying to out shout the train. It's so loud I can barely hear her. I stop moving because I don't want to upset her and because she is holding me so tightly it hurts. The train is still coming.

"We have to move!" I shout in her ear, but my baby voice disappears into the train whistle.

"Bye, baby." She whispers it, but I can still hear her. The train is almost on top of us. She sets me down and steps back. She stands there, holding my brother's hand as they both watch me crying by myself on the tracks.

My eyes fly open just before the train flattens my snotty little face into a messed up pancake. I read somewhere that if you die in a dream you're dead. How could they know that? Who could have told them?

Anyway, seeing as my eyes beat the train, I guess I'm still alive. Not so sure if that's a good thing or not any more.

"Hi Sadie."

"Cecilia." Now I'm even less sure. I guess she's here to tell me where to go. Literally.

"How are you feeling?"

Now there's an intelligent question. Last time I talked to Cecilia I found out that my mother decided she likes sons better than daughters. Since then I totally screwed up my already unbelievably screwed up life. Now I'm lying in a hospital bed with a sumo wrestler sitting on my head and bruises the size of frying pans all over my chest. I went out without permission to party with people without brains who tried to kill me by getting us attacked by an angry train. They're all lying in hospital beds, too, probably with worse injuries than mine, which should make me feel bad, but it really doesn't. I know that makes me sound like an ice cube, but I barely know any of them, and I'm not going to be wasting any tears over their problems. They all made the choice to screw up just like I did. So, how am I feeling? I have no idea how I'm feeling. I would prefer not to feel anything at all, if it's all the same to anyone.

"Just great." I don't look at her. I stare at the ceiling. It's very white. Everything here is white, like I'm in a medical snowstorm. Hospitals should try using a little color. Might make people feel better. I would paint this room black with grey stripes. Rhiannon would go more for neon pink and bright purple with little red hearts. Not that she's likely to do anything stupid enough to land herself in a place like this.

"That's good," she answers. She's either ignoring my sarcasm or is too dense to notice. "The doctor says you're doing well, and we can check you out this morning."

"Check me out? The doctor was already in checking me."

"No, Sadie. I mean we can take you out of the hospital. The others have to stay in longer. I don't know how long. But you're good to go."

I don't know why she's talking about the others. I didn't ask about them. I really don't want to know. I'm good to go? Glad she thinks so. I don't feel good to go anywhere or to do anything. I feel lousy. I don't want to go. I don't have anywhere to go. I don't want to stay, either. I just want to close my eyes and disappear once and for all so I don't have to deal any more. I'm tired.

"Sadie, did you hear me? You've been cleared to go home. I'm going to drop you off on my way to the office."

Maybe she can drop me off a cliff.

"Earth to Sadie. Are you in there? Maybe I should get a doctor."

I turn to look at her, but I still can't seem to find a way to ask her the question that is pinning me down to the bed. I just look at her for a second and then totally mortify myself by starting to cry. I can feel the tears sliding down my cheeks. They're probably red with rust because I haven't used my tear ducts in so long. My nose starts to run, too, and I sniff pathetically. People on TV always look so dramatic and beautiful when they cry. They never have snot dripping off their chin.

"Oh, honey. It's going to be OK!" Cecilia grabs me a Kleenex and hands it to me. She sits on the edge of the bed and kind of pats me on the back. I must look unbelievably pathetic for her to do that. She knows how I feel about being touched. And I'm pretty sure she never called me honey before.

I try to stop the mess coming out of my face, but I can't seem to do it. It's like all these tears were stored away in a safe, and they built up until they blew the lock. I want to suck them back in and dry my eyes, but the accident must have added to my already damaged brain because now I can't control my head.

The waterworks keep on going for what seems like forever. By the time they finally stop, the sumo wrestler is pounding both fists into my brain and my eyes hurt. I want to sleep.

"I guess you needed a good cry," Cecilia says, handing me another tissue. She calls that a good cry. What would a bad cry look like then?

"Whatever."

"Oh, so you can still talk. I was starting to worry." She sort of smiles at me. I don't smile back. Pretty sure all that crying damaged any smile muscles I might have left, not that I feel like smiling at her anyway.

"So, what now?" It's as close as I can come to asking. Even that sticks in my throat, so it comes out sounding like I'm trying to grind up a mouthful of gravel.

"We check with the nurse one more time and make sure everything's in order, and then we get you dressed and ready to go."

She just isn't going to make this easy for me. I take a deep breath, trying to find the question buried in the mess I've made of my life.

"Where?" It comes out louder than I expected, like I'm shouting it in her face. She looks a little startled and confused at the same time. I'd apologize for yelling, except that I'm not sorry.

"Where? You mean where are you going?" Is she trying to make me lose it completely, or is she just plain stupid?

"Yeah." I'm loud again. I'm not sorry again.

"Sadie. You're going back to the Kerrys'. I didn't realize that you didn't understand that. Is there a problem? Do you not want to go?" She still looks confused, or maybe that's the way she's always looked. Cow eyes all clouded up with doubt.

Do I not want to go? That's not the question here, is it? Where I want to go has never been the question. The question has always been, do they want me to come? And the answer has usually been a loud NO in capital letters. That much I can spell.

"Do they know?"

"Do they know what?" Come on! An actual cow would be more help here.

"That I'm coming! Do they know that I am coming back into their house? Did you warn them?"

"Warn them that you're coming back? Well, I let them know it would be sometime today, but I didn't give them the precise time." I am going to kick her all the way back to the farm. She's deliberately making this harder.

"Do they know they don't have to take me? That I'm returnable?" Can I make it any clearer?

Cecilia looks at me for a moment, and kind of sighs and shakes her head.

"I'm sorry. I didn't realize that's what you were asking about. I must be preoccupied today!" Or just stupid.

"You didn't answer."

"Yes, they know. I told you they don't 'return' kids once they take them in unless they have to. They don't have to send you off anywhere, and they don't want to."

"Are you sure?" This makes no sense. The pattern is all messed up and everything's out of alignment. I know how it works. Go to a placement. Get used to it. Try to fit in even when you don't. Try to relax and pretend it's going to last a while. Totally screw it all up and start all over again.

"I'm sure. I just got off the phone with Lily. Ms. Kerry, I mean."

"I know who Lily is."

"OK. Well, Lily called me to ask when you would be ready and asked if I could pick you up because Rhiannon's at school and Brad's at work, so the little ones would need a sitter if she had to come for you."

"I don't understand." Maybe I'm not ready to go home. Maybe my head isn't working at all any more and I can't understand English. Or any other language.

"You're going home, Sadie."

"Home? Back to the Kerrys'?"

"Yes. And once you're settled a little, I think we need to talk more about your family. I know you have things to sort out. You can also talk to Ms. Kerry about it if you want to. She's a pretty good listener from what I understand."

"But I messed up." I don't care about my imaginary family and I don't need to talk. I just need to understand why the Kerry family still wants me back.

"Oh yeah, you definitely messed up. Even though you had an extremely valid reason to feel upset, you still made some really bad choices and paid a pretty scary price. I'm sure the Kerrys will have some words for you and some clear rules."

"But they want me to come back." I can't get past that one fact.

"They do. But if we keep talking about it instead of doing it, you might end up stuck in here another night. Can you get yourself dressed?"

"Yes!" I pull the blanket up around my neck as if I think she's going to strip me down and dress me up like a doll. She laughs at me and gets up.

"OK, relax. I'll wait out in the hall and you get yourself organized. Then we'll head home, OK?"

Home. She keeps saying that. It's not really true. It's not really my home. It's Rhiannon's home and her parents' home and even Adam's and Chandra's and the superbrats'.

I'm just a visitor.

Right?

chapter 31

"Wrong. One hundred percent. I told you that when you came to us. Walk through that door with your bag in hand, and this becomes your home for as long as you need it to be."

I'm sitting on the couch at the Kerry house. Ms. K is sitting beside me and the superbrats are down for a nap. Though they're not really napping because I can hear one of them complaining loudly and the other one singing even louder. Now I know I'm back.

"You sure sounded piss...I mean, angry, with me when you were in the hospital that night."

"Of course I was angry. You took a really foolish risk. You knew that boy had been drinking but you still got in the car with him. You're a smart kid and you know the way things are. You knew better."

"Yeah. I just wanted a break. To get out and do something different or whatever."

"Without telling me and without using your brain."

"I messed up."

"Absolutely." She looks at me. She doesn't look angry now. She doesn't look happy, either. She just looks like Ms. K.

"Now what happens?"

"What happens now is that we have to talk about this and come to some agreements about how things work around here. I know you don't like rules much, but I do. Everyone in this house is expected to follow them to the best of their ability. Which, in your case, is considerable."

"What do you do if someone just doesn't follow the rules in this house?" I'm not looking at her.

"You're asking me if I would make the someone leave?"

"Whatever."

"So, if Rhiannon doesn't follow the rules you figure I should ask her to go live elsewhere?"

"No, of course not! She's your kid. Though some parents kick out their biokids, too."

"That's a true statement and a pretty sad one. Regardless of what some parents do, I believe that you make a commitment when you take someone into your home, biologically or otherwise. They mess up, you help them to find a way to avoid doing it again."

"And what if they do it again?"

"I guess you just keep trying. Do you want to leave here? Is that why you 'messed up'?"

"No. If I wanted to leave I'd just say so." At least, I think I would. I mean, I have no trouble telling people what I want. If I want to leave, I'll just say so. I think. Maybe.

"Do you like it here?"

"Sure. I guess. I mean, it's different than other places and the super...the little kids are kind of a lot to take. But no one's mean to me or anything if that's what you mean."

"I'm glad to hear that. But I assumed that was the case, and I would expect you to tell me if it wasn't. I was actually asking if you're starting to feel at all comfortable here and if you feel you can stay."

Good question, but I'm not so sure if there's a good answer. Am I comfortable? What does that even mean? This couch is comfortable, all worn down and squishy so that I can slide down into the cushions and just chill. Is living here comfortable? Can I slide down into it and feel relaxed?

"I don't know if I'm exactly comfortable. It's pretty intense around here and everyone is really interested in everything I do. I'm not used to that."

"Fair enough. We can't back off on rules and expectations but we can back off a little on personal things. Is that what you want?"

I don't say anything because I'm not sure what to say. Do I want them to back off? I thought I did. I thought I was sick of sappy land and everyone always telling me how great I am. It does make me uncomfortable, like I'm walking around in someone else's skin and it's too tight for me. But do I want them to back off or do I want to try to get used to it? Do I want to talk to Ms. K about all the stuff Cecilia told me about my mother and brother? Will she even care? Do I even care? This is crazy. I always used to know exactly what I wanted and how I felt. Now I don't seem to have any mind of my own left at all. Maybe that train hit me harder than everyone thought.

"Well, judging from the silence and assuming you're thinking rather than ignoring me, we'll just decide you need some time to think. If you want to talk to me about anything I'm ready to listen. But right now *I* think you're tired and you might want to get some rest before Rhiannon comes home. She's been pretty worried. I'm not too sure I can tell her to back off at the moment and, also, just a warning…"

"What?"

"When Rhiannon is worried, she talks more than usual!" Ms. K grins at me and my mouth grins back without asking my permission.

I crawl up the stairs and back into my bed with the big warm comforter and try to sleep so I can deal with Rhiannon's mouth when it gets home with her from school. It's only been a couple of days, but I'm sure she'll have about three hours' worth of news to catch me up on. My eyes are closed but my mind is open. I'm trying to make sense of this, but it's new ground and I don't know how to figure it out.

Why are the Kerrys so stuck on keeping me around? They made this big commitment to me without knowing me at all. Which isn't the confusing part. The confusing part is that they're sticking to it. At least so far. Why are they doing this if my own mother wouldn't?

I'm not sure I know how to do this. Let myself be comfortable in this house and believe that I can stay until I want to go. I don't know if I *can* do this.

"Sadie! Mom said you were lying down and I should be quiet so I'm whispering just in case you're asleep but I just wanted to say that I'm really glad you're home."

"It's OK. I'm not asleep." I open my eyes to look at her.

"Oh good! Because I have so much to tell you! Everyone is talking about the accident. The other kids are still in hospital, did you know that? Tom is hurt really bad, and so is Grace. Jeremy and Tony were hurt worse than you but not as bad as Tom and Grace.

You missed so much at school today and everyone was asking about you and the accident and my mom was so worried about you but mad at you at the same time and I was just worried but mad at myself so I couldn't concentrate in science class, which I guess is bad news for both of us because I was planning on getting you your notes so you wouldn't fall behind and..."

Her voice chatters on and my eyes start to close again. This time, the sound of her voice manages to silence everything else in my head. I finally feel myself drifting off to sleep. My last thought is to wonder if Rhiannon will even notice.

When I open my eyes again, it's dark and quiet in the room. I can hear the even sound of Rhiannon's breathing. Did she actually talk herself to sleep or have I been out so long that she went to bed? I reach out to the clock on the table beside my bed. Two o'clock. I guess I was tired.

Now I'm hungry, too, though. The hospital food was worse than gross, and I didn't eat anything there. I passed out before I had anything here, either. My stomach is dancing and if I don't feed it, I won't get any more sleep. I could always wake Rhiannon up and get her to talk me back to sleep, but that hardly seems fair.

I slide carefully out of bed and tiptoe down the hall. No one is making a sound. Even the rugrats are quiet for a change. Guess their afternoon nap wore them out. I try to keep my feet from making any sound, either, because everyone around here seems to sleep with their doors open. I have no trouble finding my way, because there is always a night-light on in the hallway. I start to slip past Adam's room, but for some reason I peek in. He's there, all curled up in a ball, sleeping like a baby. Kind of looks like one too. A really, really big one.

The next room is the superbrats', so I'm extra quiet. Chandra does not bunk with them, which is nice for her. Although, they do look almost human lying there with their dirty little thumbs stuck in their finally quiet mouths. Chandra's room is actually downstairs off the kitchen. It's a really tiny room but it's a single. The Kerrys turned some sun porch or something into a room when they got an extra kid one time. Or something like that. I don't remember. The information was buried in one of Rhiannon's longer speeches.

The Kerrys' room is the last one. Their door is open, too, which is really surprising, because you would think they'd want their privacy after dealing with all these kids all day. Including me. Maybe especially me right now. I know I shouldn't but I take a quick look in anyway. Mr. K is there, snoring away, buried in the covers. I can't see Ms. K. Maybe she buried herself even deeper than he did. I kind of want to go in and make sure she's there.

The feeling gives me this strange sense of déjà vu.

I creep the rest of the way down the hall and start my way down the stairs. No one is going to hear me now, but I still try to keep it completely silent. I make it through the living room. There isn't a night-light in here, but I don't want to turn on a lamp in case I bother someone. So I have to step carefully to make sure I don't land on a loud and obnoxious toy of any description.

My stomach is growling so loudly I'm sure it's going to wake up the whole house. I hope there's something quick and easy to eat in the fridge. I make it across the treacherous territory of the living room rug without incident and manage to push open the kitchen door.

"Well, hi. Are you hungry?" I just about fall over on my

wounded head at the sight of Ms. K sitting at the kitchen table having a cup of tea.

"Actually, yeah. Is it OK if I get something to eat?" I kind of feel like I got caught stealing cookies or something.

"Sure. I was just having a cup of herbal tea. Would you like some?" She gets up and starts bustling around making me tea. Before I can say anything, she's also making me a sandwich. I'm not sure what to do here.

"Sadie. Sit down. You look like you might keel over. I'm making you something to eat."

"You don't have to. I can…"

"Just sit down. I'm a little hungry too. Supper was busy. I think I might have forgotten to eat." She's looking at me with her Ms. K eyes so I do what she says, even though it feels weird.

So here I am, doing the last possible thing I could ever have imagined doing the night after almost killing myself with my own stupidity. I'm sitting eating grilled cheese sandwiches and drinking some kind of tea that tastes like candy canes at two thirty in the morning with a woman who should really be standing over me watching me pack my bags. We don't really talk about much. We mostly just chew and sip.

Maybe it doesn't feel so weird after all.

Maybe it feels kind of nice.

Maybe this is what comfortable feels like?

chapter 32

"Everyone is staring at me."

We're back at school. Ms. K thought I should wait a few more days to make sure I'm totally fine, but I just want life to get back to normal. Not that anything in my life is ever exactly normal, but going to school is better than sitting around like an invalid at home. Besides, the house is full of screaming rugrats all day and if I stay home too long I'm afraid Ms. K will ask me to help her with them and I'd feel like I had to and then I'd have to kill one of them and then I'd be back in another mess. Or something like that. Maybe I s*hould* move out of the Kerrys'. The inside of my head sounds more like Rhiannon every day!

"Yeah, well, you guys have been the main source of conversation around here for the past few days. Not much exciting happens in this town. Not that I'm excited that you got hit by a train, but other people sure are. Everyone is gossiping about Tom and whether he was drunk and Grace and whether she was Tom's girlfriend for the night, although I'm not sure what that has to do with the accident. Do you know how they're doing, by the way?"

"No, I only know what you tell me." Everyone seems to think I should know what's going on with these four strangers. I know I shared this big horrible experience with them and everything, but I don't actually know any of them. A few short almost-conversations at the dumpster and one disaster of a party don't make for a lasting relationship.

"I heard that he might be paralyzed. I don't know if it's true, but that's what everyone is saying."

"Well, everyone doesn't know what they're talking about. I'm sure he'll be fine. Guys like that are always fine."

"I also heard that Grace's face is all scarred up from that old windshield shattering. Everyone says that she's going to have to have plastic surgery to put her face back together."

"I don't know about that, either. I guess it's possible. She seems pretty tough. She'll deal with it." I actually have no idea whether she will deal with it or not. I don't even know if it's true. I heard she got cut up, but I didn't know how badly. She might think a few scars are cool. She's put enough holes all over her own body already.

"I guess so. Anyway, I have geography so I'll see you later. Are you going to Jackson's or the cafeteria at lunch?"

"Haven't decided. Probably Jackson's, though. Fewer people gawking at me and less chance someone will work up the nerve to actually ask me questions." So far no one has. I haven't exactly opened myself up for friendly chatting around here, and no one can figure out how to approach me. A couple of the overly made-up squad sort of took a step or two toward me outside the English room, but I stared them down and they backed off. Wilson looked like he was going to say something brilliantly stupid when I walked in the room, but I stared him down, too, and he backed off. Maybe the accident gave me new superpowers. Maybe I have laser eyes now like Sandi and can fry people who bug me like mosquitoes on a zapper.

"OK, well, I'll see you later. Don't worry about all the people though if you come eat with me. I'll protect you from all the meanies!" Rhiannon laughs and runs down the hall. Five-foot-nothing and about as tough as a kitten. I feel very protected.

I've only been out of school a few days so I'm not too far behind. At least not much further than usual. I'm always behind, but it doesn't matter because this is one race I don't care about winning. All I want to do is survive it for two more years so I can get out and start some sort of life. Get a job and an apartment and some privacy.

Ms. K reminded me again yesterday that I can stay with them even longer than two years if I want to. I can go to postsecondary school and live at "home." Or I can even stay with them after I have my first job until I get settled. That's what she said. I'm still not sure she will still be saying it a year from now if I take her up on it.

Pretty sure I'm stuck having to live somewhere for the next two years at least. Getting myself attacked by a large train didn't really help my cause with Cecilia. Not that she's said anything about it, but I figure the whole cutting-me-loose-at-sixteen plan is pretty much history by this point. It was already the longest of long shots and I just blew it right out of the park. Made her tell me all about my pathetic family life for nothing.

Don't think my mother's looking for anything but a five-minute reunion so she doesn't have to feel guilty about picking my

brother instead of me. Do druggy loser mothers who hate their
daughters feel guilty?

So that leaves me with the Kerrys or finding another group
home. Foster homes are pretty scarce for kids my age. No one
really wants to let a screwed-up teenager into their house. If they
have kids, they're afraid we're going to be a negative influence on
their little darlings. If they don't have kids, they're usually looking
for one, and someone my age doesn't really count as a kid.

Someone my age is mostly a problem.

"Sadie! I'm glad to see you. How are you doing?" I chose Jackson's
for lunchtime. We're standing in her rat maze at the back of the
classroom. Rhiannon will be disappointed, but she'll get over it as
soon as she finds someone willing to listen to her talk.

"I'm mostly OK." Not sure if that's true or not, but close
enough.

"I'm glad to hear that. I was so worried when I heard about the
accident. I was happy to hear that you weren't too badly hurt, and
I understand now that Tony and Jeremy have also been released
from hospital. I'm keeping Grace and Tom in my prayers."

I don't know what to say to that. I don't pray. I used to pretend
to pray when I lived with Sampson so she thought I was repenting
all my ten-year-old sins. I never did see the point to talking to an
imaginary person up on an imaginary throne somewhere in the
sky. If I remember correctly, this guy that Sampson prayed to was
pretty angry all of the time and apparently spent most of his time
figuring out ways to punish fosterkids.

"Do you know how they are?" I don't know why I'm asking.
Everyone seems to be expecting me to already know.

"Grace is still in hospital," Jackson says, her voice sounding so sad that I'm not sure if I want to hear the rest. "She's pretty badly injured. Severe lacerations to her face and a broken collar bone and a couple of broken ribs. She's going to need surgery." She stops for a second and closes her eyes, shaking her head a little. When she opens them, they're shiny and a bit red.

"And Tom?"

"We don't know all the details but he's having a very tough time. He didn't have his seat belt on and he was thrown from the car as it fell from the bridge. His neck was damaged and it doesn't look very positive for him." A tear sneaks out of her left eye. I stare at it as it rolls down her cheek. I've never seen a teacher cry before. She sniffs a little and wipes her face. She looks at her hand like she's surprised that it's wet.

"Sorry. I just get so upset when kids hurt themselves. And for nothing!"

"He'll be OK eventually, though. He's a tough guy." She looks at me and smiles. I've never seen a smile quite like that before. It's sadder looking than the tear.

"I don't know. As I said, we don't have all the details, but right now they think he might be paralyzed. I don't know if that's permanent or how extensive. But I do know his life will never be the same."

I nod a little as if I understand, and head over to my usual computer to pretend to do some work. Staring at the screen, I wonder about Tom. I haven't given him much thought. I guess I should feel sorry for him. But really, I hardly knew the guy. And what I did know about him didn't exactly make me want to be anyone in his life. Players who think they're demi-gods are not my style.

I'm thinking about him now, though. I try to imagine him,

tall and too attractive for his own good and all buff from hanging out at the demi-god gym. I try to imagine him in a wheelchair with useless legs or even useless arms and legs. I can't imagine it. It's too bizarre and like something out a bad TV movie, the kind that they make just to depress people.

I don't know what to feel about him. I mean, it was his idea to drive across the tracks in front of a train. Well, it was Tony or Jeremy who said it first, but Tom wasn't far behind. He was the one who got half-pissed and decided to drive across town. Even if he did know the route with his eyes shut, he probably shouldn't have tried to drive it that way. He should have taken the underpass. He should have decided to stay sober. He should have stopped when he saw that big-ass train coming toward us. He should have never asked me to come to the stupid party in the first place.

I should be really mad at him. He almost killed me.

I should feel really sorry for him. I'm walking around and he isn't.

Mostly, I don't feel anything.

chapter 33

"So, did you hear that Grace got out of the hospital? Do you want to go see her with me?" Rhiannon asks me a few days later. I'm not sure I heard her right.

Why would she want to go see Grace? I thought Grace had tormented her since they were rugrats together in elementary school.

"Why?"

"Well, you went to the party with her and everything. I thought you were friends. Especially now, after what you went through together."

"I don't think getting almost killed together is a real bonding experience. I barely know her. I haven't talked to her since the accident. I barely talked to her before. Not sure I want to see her now."

"Oh. Well, I thought she might want to see you. I don't think she has tons of friends any more. She used to but now mostly she hangs with those guys and they probably won't come. Well, Tom can't." Her voice gets kind of quiet and trails off. We both sit there for a minute thinking about Tom. At least I assume she is. He still can't walk and isn't doing much with his arms. No one seems to know if it's permanent or not. Or they're not telling us. I guess it's none of my business, anyway.

"I don't think she'd want to see me. Or you. I didn't think you were ever friends."

"No, we're pretty much the opposite. But she's having a terrible time and she might need to see that people care about her. I've known her for a long time and I do care what happens to her even though she's kind of mean most of the time. I know she has her reasons for acting the way she does even if I don't like it much. I doubt she'll give me a hard time if I come visit her now when she's feeling so lousy herself. We can bring flowers or something."

"Flowers? What would she want with flowers?" Rhiannon laughs at me.

"Sadie, sometimes I think you come from another planet! People like flowers when they don't feel well. Like the ones sitting on your dresser." She points to a vase filled with yellow daisies. I did notice it sitting there, but I thought they were Rhiannon's. It never even occurred to me that someone put them there for me.

"Anyway, I don't know if I feel OK about going to Grace's house. I don't even know where she lives." As if that's going to work.

"Oh, I do. She's lived in the same house her whole life. I know exactly where it is." Of course Rhiannon knows exactly where Grace lives. She probably knows where everyone in town lives. Doesn't change the fact that visiting Grace is pretty close to the last thing I want to do.

So why is it that two hours later I find myself wandering

down the sidewalk beside Rhiannon, who is marching along like she's the commander of some kind of army for stupid people who can't seem to control their own lives? I don't know how Rhiannon does it. I mean she's such a mini-person and it seems like she's filled with nothing but bubbly air made up of happy thoughts, but somehow she manages to be strong enough to push me into doing things I don't want to do and saying things I don't want to say. Maybe I'm the one filled with air, only mine wouldn't be bubbly. It would be the hot kind made up of empty thoughts.

Grace's house is just a couple of blocks away from the school, so we get there much too fast for my liking. I don't know if Rhiannon has even called over there first to warn them that we're invading their space, waging war on their privacy. I don't want to ask her, because I'm not sure I want to hear the answer. I'll just go into this ignorant. It's one of my best qualities, anyway.

Her house is on a street I don't remember seeing before. The houses are all attached to one another, rows of identical doors and windows lined up in single file. A few of the doors try to break the mold by changing color or adding a wreath of flowers. The front lawns, if you can even call them that, are tiny. Some of the lawns have even tinier gardens stuck in the middle of them, filled with brown plants withering in the cold. Grace's house is in the middle of the row. There's no garden here. There is a bucket full of sand sitting beside the cement step with dozens of old cigarette butts in it. There's also a row of beer bottles sitting along the wall, which I think is a nicer decorating touch than flowers.

"Subsidized housing," Rhiannon says like she's explaining something to me.

"What?"

"Oh, I saw you kind of staring at the houses and thought you were wondering about them. This block is where all the subsidized housing units in town are. You know, the houses for people who can't actually afford a house so they get one with government funding or whatever. Grace's dad has had something wrong with his back for a long time and can't work, and her mom has trouble finding a job that pays much so they've always lived here."

"Yeah, I know what subsidized housing is. Lived in a few. Man, do you know this much about everybody in town?" A walking, talking encyclopedia of personal information that people probably don't want her to know.

Rhiannon's still marching, so she doesn't answer. She heads right up to the door without breaking pace. I lag behind, bad little soldier that I am. I'm hoping that no one is home.

"What can I do for you?" The door has opened before I even finish hoping and a woman is standing there, not looking too happy to see us. She has a uniform of some kind on, not sure what it's for, but she's obviously either on her way to work or just coming home. Either way she probably isn't thrilled to find our pathetic little army standing on her doorstep.

"Hi Mrs. Miller. You remember me. I'm Rhiannon Kerry. Grace and I go to school together. This is Sadie. She's a friend of Grace's. She was actually there the night of the accident. We're here to say hi to Grace and to give her these." She holds out a little bunch of multi-colored flowers that we bought on the way. Grace's mom looks at them and kind of sniffs, like they smell bad. I'm with her. Flowers are so sickeningly sweet. I thought I was going to keel over in that store. Kind of wish I had. Then I'd be passed out among the posies instead of standing here looking stupid.

"She's not feeling too hot. Face is a mess. She's just lying around feeling sorry for herself. I told her she should just get up and figure out what she's going to do next. She can't just stay at home all of the time." She's talking really loudly as if she's trying to make sure the neighbors know her business. You wouldn't have to actually be all that loud around here to share your deepest darkest secrets with the person attached to your wall.

"Can we see her for a few minutes? Maybe seeing friends will help her feel like getting up." Rhiannon is still smiling sweetly and holding out the flowers. Mrs. Miller looks at her like she's a fly that she'd like to swat. Rhiannon just keeps on smiling. I'm staying back, ready to run just in case Ms. M has a really big fly swatter hidden anywhere.

"Oh, all right. Grace! There's people here to see you. Get your sorry ass out of bed and come down here." She's yelling up the stairs as we slide into the front hall. Rhiannon slips right on past her.

"It's OK, we'll head up. She's probably tired." She hustles up the stairs before anyone can say anything. I run up behind her. I'm not staying down here alone. I can take care of myself and all, but Grace's mom looks like she might try to take me on just for sport. I'm still a little weak from my big trauma and all, so I think I'll pass on this one.

I get a quick glance around at the house as I chase Rhiannon up the stairs. Messy like the Kerrys', but in a different way. There aren't any toys lying around. But there's pretty much everything else you could imagine. Papers and clothes and food containers and dishes and bottles seem to be decorating every surface that I can see in the thirty seconds I manage to look.

The house smells like dirty socks and cigarettes. The smell gives me a flashback to a house I lived in a few years back, and for just a second I expect to see my ex-pseudomother standing at the top of the stairs, yelling that I'm late home from school.

Rhiannon heads to the second door of the row of three closed doors. Not sure how she knows which one belongs to Grace. At least she knocks.

"Come in." The voice is faint and doesn't sound much like Grace. I wonder if we've come to the wrong room after all. Rhiannon opens the door carefully and walks in.

"Hi Grace. We just wanted to come and check on you and bring you these." She holds up the flowers. The room is small and feels warm and stuffy the minute you walk in. There's a small dresser painted pink and a desk painted black, which looks more like a Grace color. Or is black a non-color? The floor is covered in clothes, like Rhiannon's side of our room, but there aren't any books, which is more like my side of our room. There's a small bed by the window with a blanket-covered lump in the middle of it. The lump moves a little when we walk in, but doesn't turn around.

"Who is it?"

"It's me, Rhiannon. And Sadie's here, too." She gestures to me to come closer and kind of points at my mouth like she wants me to talk.

"Hi Grace."

"Why are you here?" the lump asks, voice muffled by the blankets that are wrapped tight like a cocoon. I look at Rhiannon, who looks back at me and gestures again. My turn again? I just went.

"It's like she said. We just wanted to check on you. See how you are." I didn't want to check on her. I was bullied into it by my drill sergeant. The lump shifts a little more and it looks like she's trying to roll over. I'm not sure if she's rolling toward us or away.

"I'm lousy. Now you know. Bye."

"Oh, Grace. I'm so sorry this happened to you. It must be so

hard to deal with all of this. Is there anything we can do for you?"
Rhiannon steps into the room a little more.

"You can piss off."

Sounds like a plan to me. I shrug my shoulders and turn to
leave. Rhiannon grabs my arm and pulls me back. She is the only
person on earth who could get away with that and still keep her
hand. I'm starting to get how tough she really is underneath all
those happy thoughts.

"Grace. We'll go if you want us to. We just wanted you to
know that lots of people at school are worried about you and want
you to come back."

The room is quiet for a moment or two. The lump moves
around on the bed until it turns into a person. Grace gets up really
slowly, her back to us as she pushes herself into a sitting position.

"You don't want to see me. We're not even friends. I treat you
like crap."

"That's true. But I still don't like that you got hurt and I guess
I wanted you to know that. We almost didn't come because Sadie
wasn't sure coming was the right thing because…. Well, Sadie,
you explain it to her."

Me? Explain what? That someone half my size had managed
to force me here against my will?

"I just didn't want to get in your face. Thought you'd want your
privacy." Lame, but the best I can do under pressure.

"My face? Are you trying to be funny?"

"Funny? No! I'm never funny. I didn't mean anything by that.
I wasn't thinking about your actual face." I look at Rhiannon,
pleading for help. She doesn't seem to know what to say, either.
For the first time in her life.

"I don't have an actual face anymore. I have a freaking scar festival where I used to have skin. I'm a monster. They don't even know how much they can fix because it isn't all covered by insurance and my parents have no money. Not that they'd pay even if they had it."

"Grace, you're not a monster. You had an accident. It wasn't your fault."

Grace turns around and looks at us for the first time. Her face looks like she was attacked by a grizzly bear, covered in angry, ugly scratches and cuts. Her one eye is covered by a bandage that reaches down over most of one side of her face. Her other eye is bright red and looks like it would cry tears of blood if you upset her too much. I can't think of anything to say.

"Oh, Grace. I'm so so sorry. It must be so painful." Rhiannon goes right over to the bed and sits down beside her, right up close and personal. She looks Grace directly in the "good" eye and holds one of her hands. I wonder if she went to some special school that teaches people the exact right thing to do when someone is upset. I don't know how she figures it out. I always end up doing the exact wrong thing. Like now. I just stand there, gawking like an idiot, which would be exactly what Grace would be afraid people would do.

"It does really hurt. I'm supposed to have prescription pain-killers, but they're too expensive. Mom says I'm just being weak, and I have to snap out of it. I can't even get a drink to help take the edge off because dad keeps it all locked away for himself, and I'm too weak to get around him."

"I wish I could do something to help," Rhiannon says, still kind of patting her on the hand. This is one of the kids who's called Rhiannon every name in the book and a few that are probably not in any books. She's spent years making Rhiannon's life miserable, and now that her own life is miserable, all Rhiannon can do is try to help her. I don't get it.

"Sadie?" Grace's red eye turns to look for me. I step forward a bit.

"Yeah?"

"Can you do me a favor?"

"Sure." I can't believe Rhiannon got me into this.

"Can you go see Tom for me and tell him I'm OK. He kind of likes you. Not in a guy-girl way or anything. Not the way he likes me. Liked me, I mean."

"He still likes you, Grace," Rhiannon says, looking at me.

"No one will ever like me again with this face. Even if they try to fix it, it won't be the same." She closes her eye. I don't want her to cry. I don't want to see if it actually leaks blood. Why does she want me to go? Rhiannon would be much better at this than me. I open my mouth to suggest it and Rhiannon punches me in the arm. Actually punches me! She has sharp little knuckles, too. I'm so amazed that she hit me that my mouth snaps shut. When it opens again, Rhiannon seems to have control over me because all of the wrong words come out.

"I guess I can try, but I don't know if I can. He's still in the hospital and I don't know the rules." Hopefully the rule is that I can't go. I don't think I can handle it.

"He can have visitors now. I talked to Jeremy and he told me. He told me to call Tom myself but I'm afraid to."

"He can't see you over the phone," I say helpfully.

"Not that it would matter because he will still like you even if you're hurt," Rhiannon says, a lot more helpfully. She glares at me and I step back in case she decides to hit me again. She does it too often, I might have to retaliate. Then I'd be moving out!

"I just don't think I can talk to him right now. But I just want him to know I'm thinking about him. And that I don't blame him. And that I hope he gets better. Can you tell him, Sadie?"

"Yeah, I'll tell him." I'm pretty sure I'm lying, but it seems like a good time to use that particular skill.

"Thanks. I have to sleep now. My mom is going to be up here soon telling me to get out of bed and clean the house. She tells me that every day, but I haven't done it yet. One of these days, she's just going to drag me out though, so I have to be ready. Once I'm out of this bed, I'm right out of this house living somewhere without parents." She puts her hand to the side of her face and touches it. Then she rolls herself back up into her cocoon and turns back into a lump.

Rhiannon and I go back downstairs. We're walking this time and can see the house a bit more clearly. I can hear a TV blaring from the living room. A man who must be her dad is flaked out on the couch, sipping on a beer and smoking. Her mom is standing beside him, yelling at him to get up off the couch and help her make supper.

We leave without them noticing us. We walk home, both of us quiet for once, disappearing into our own thoughts. I don't know what Rhiannon is thinking. I'm not totally sure what I'm thinking, either. Grace has lived with her bioparents her whole life, and they treat her like she shouldn't be taking the time to get better in her own bed. Even all banged up like that, all she can think about is getting out of her house, away from her parents. I can't blame her, either.

Bet my mother's just like Mrs. Miller. My brother's probably planning to move out first chance he gets.

I look over at Rhiannon, wondering what she thinks about

Grace's parents. Could she find something nice to say about them? Wonder what Rhiannon would think if I told her about my mother. Could she find something nice to say about someone who dumps one kid and keeps the other one?

I don't ask her, though. I don't feel like talking. Apparently, and amazingly, she doesn't, either. I wonder if she knows that she's still holding Grace's flowers?

chapter 34

"Today? Are you sure about this? Did you check with anyone?"

"Yes, I asked my mom to call the hospital for us. He's allowed visitors. Some other kids from school have already gone."

"I don't know about this. I barely know him. Lots of other girls know him a lot better. We could find someone else to give him Grace's message. Or maybe you could talk her into calling him herself."

"She's too messed up right now. She asked you to do it. I guess it's because you were in the car with them and that makes her feel close to you. I really think you have to do this for her."

"I really don't know why I have to do anything for her. I don't owe her anything. I didn't put her in the car or in that bed. None of this is my fault."

"I didn't say it was or even think it was! Of course it isn't your fault. It's no one's fault. It was just an accident."

"That's not totally true, though, is it?" Rhiannon looks at

248

me. I don't really want to talk about this, but she's pushing me. "Everyone is feeling so sorry for poor Tom. He's all messed up and in a wheelchair, and he might never get out of it. I understand that and I agree it's not good. I guess I wish things were different for him."

"You guess you wish it?"

"It wasn't really an accident, was it? I mean, it was an accident because I don't think anyone wanted the train to hit us, but it *was* someone's fault. I don't know why everyone's acting like it wasn't just because Tom got hurt. If he was OK, everyone would be blaming him like he deserves."

"That doesn't seem fair with him still sitting in the hospital."

"That's my point. Poor Tom sitting in the hospital. But he's the one who drank at the party, and he's the one who decided to play chicken with a train. Poor Tom should have used his brain, and he wouldn't be in this mess. Grace wouldn't be hiding in her bedroom with that pathetic excuse for a mother getting on her case. The other guys wouldn't have been all banged up." I stop for breath. Too many words.

"What about you?"

"What about me? I'm the only one who didn't get hurt. Nothing happened to me."

"You got a concussion and all those bruises. It was really scary when we heard about it. We heard the crash, you know. Everyone in town heard it. It was the loudest sound I think I ever heard. The train kept on blowing its horn over and over, and then there was this huge screeching noise and a giant bang and then..."

"I know! I was there, remember?" I put my hand up to block her words. I don't want to think about it. The sounds from that night seem to be carved right into my brain. Every time I hear the train coming through town, I feel like I have to hide so it doesn't come after me. I want to put my fingers in my ears to block out the sounds, but I know it won't work because most of what I hear is coming from the inside out.

I don't know why it's bothering me so much. I mean, I wasn't hurt like everyone else. I was just banged around a bit. It serves me right for what I did. It was my fault for lying to Ms. K and getting in that car in the first place. I could tell it was a death trap the first time I saw it. I knew Tom was a player the first time I saw him. You can't trust players.

"Sorry. I wasn't thinking. I know it must bother you."

"I just wish I could forget about it. But I can't. It's in my face all the time with everyone talking about *poor* Tom and *poor* Grace." That sounds awful even to me.

"I just wish it hadn't happened to any of you. It's all so terrible. I agree with you that Tom was stupid. Incredibly stupid. And I know you always hear these stories about the horrible things that can happen if you drink and drive, but you still don't really want it to happen to someone you know. He didn't deserve this to happen, even if it was his fault. He's still *poor* Tom even if he was stupid." Rhiannon's voice reminds me of her mother's.

"He was stupid. He almost killed all of us. I'm not sure if I want to go and see him. I think I'm too mad at him to be nice and supportive. You go and give him Grace's message, OK?"

I walk away without waiting for her answer. It's too much to ask. I can't go and look at him and try to feel sympathy for him. I know he'll look sad and pathetic. I can't in a million years imagine what it would be like to think that you might never walk again. Trapped in a wheelchair for the rest of your life. I don't have anything to say to someone in that terrible a place.

I don't want to walk into the hospital room and look at him sitting in his personal hell and only feel pissed that he hurt Grace and Tony and Jeremy.

And me.

He did hurt me. Not as badly as the others, but he still could have killed me. Not that my life is worth much, but it's still mine. Even if he didn't kill me, he still could have screwed up my life and sent me flying into another group home. It wasn't his to screw up. I can screw my own life up without any help.

Which I have probably done again by coming home by myself instead of going to the hospital. Coming home. That's what Rhiannon says every day. "Are you ready to come home?" Except she didn't say it today because she went in the opposite direction after school and will probably decide I'm such a selfish idiot that she'll never talk to me again. Which would normally be a good thing, but I'm actually getting kind of used to her nonstop sunshine-and-roses routine, and I'm wondering if I would almost kind of maybe miss it if she decided to clam up.

"And I think Rhiannon's mad at me for not going, but I just can't do it right now." I'm not sure when I developed such a big mouth. Rhiannon's mad at me, and now I'm telling her mother about it, which will probably make her mad at me, too. Life was a lot easier when I just kept it closed and hid below the surface where no one noticed me.

"I don't blame you for not feeling ready to do that. You've been through a lot that Rhiannon likely can't really understand."

Ms. K wipes the snotty nose of one of the superbrats and sends her back out to play. We're standing at the window of the kitchen, watching all the little kids try to murder each other in the back yard. I'm not sure how I started spilling my guts to her. I just came back from school on my own and when she asked me where Rhiannon was, I lost control of my mouth and it started pouring out all my thoughts like a broken faucet stuck on full power.

"You're taking *my* side?" Rhiannon's the biokid. Pseudomoms always take the biokid's side.

"There are no sides here, Sadie. Rhiannon likes to take care of people. I don't know if that's from growing up in this crazy household where she's had to get used to so many different children, or if it's just her personality. Either way, it's who she is. She was just trying to help Tom and Grace and probably you, too. Her good intentions sometimes get ahead of her thinking things through." She's not exactly dissing Rhiannon, but it still kind of sounds like she's on my side. If there were sides, that is.

"Alisha called her a collector." Why'd I tell her that? That's history and has nothing to do with right now. Maybe I should sew my mouth shut. If I knew how to sew.

"A collector? Of what?"

"Fosterkids. She told me that Rhiannon was only my friend because she felt sorry for me because I'm a fostergirl." I'm still talking. Wonder where she keeps the needles and thread. I heard a rumor I'm good at problem solving. I should be able to figure out how to stitch my lips together.

"Do you believe that?" She glances at me for a second, then goes back to looking out the window. Two of the rugrats seem to be trying to rip each other's faces off. Ms. K just watches until they break it up, but she looks poised to run out and save the day just in case someone removes a body part. It ends fast and they run off to play in the sandbox. Both of them seem to still have their own eyes and noses, so I guess they don't need a rescue operation.

"Not really. I did for a while. It's like you said, she likes to take care of people. I thought I was one of those people and that was the only reason she was hanging around with me." I shrug my shoulders so that she knows I don't really care. She doesn't notice.

"She probably did want to take care of you, especially at first. She likes to take care of me, too. And everyone else in this house. She used to take care of Alisha when she was here, even though Alisha is older than she is. Alisha doesn't remember that part, I guess. She just remembers being hurt and angry when she wanted to come back and the timing made it impossible. Rhiannon wanting to take care of you doesn't make her less of a friend, you know. It's actually the other way around."

"I guess I'm kind of starting to get that." What I'm really starting to get is that being friends with Rhiannon doesn't seem to be a choice any more. She's like a bad habit that I can't seem to break, even when I try.

Except that maybe I finally managed to break it today. She looked pretty disappointed when she left me at lunchtime, and all I saw of her after school was her back walking away from me.

"I wouldn't worry too much about her being upset with you. She isn't much of a grudge keeper. She has a strong sense of loyalty to people she cares about." I've noticed that. I've also noticed that Rhiannon is strong in lots of ways that I didn't notice at first. I think I might have a disability in people skills along with reading and writing.

"What about the Tom stuff?" I hate that I feel guilty that I didn't go with her. I never used to feel guilty about anything. I did what I wanted to do without worrying about what anyone else thought. Now I have to think about other people's feelings when I can't even find my own.

"You will figure that one out when you're ready. It's a pretty confusing situation, and I think you're entitled to some time to decide how you feel about it and about him. Rhiannon will give him the message. She'll probably give him all kinds of messages." She smiles.

"Yeah, she never runs out of things to say." I smile too, my muscles creaking a little as they try to move my face up. Rhiannon does that to people. She makes you smile even when she isn't there and even when you don't think you have anything to smile about. I'm pretty sure I've always had the exact opposite effect on people.

"I'm glad *you're* starting to find a few things to say."

"Yeah, well, it feels a little weird. I'm not much for talking about myself."

"I've noticed. You can talk to me whenever you want. And you don't have to talk when you don't want. At least to me. Rhiannon is a different story."

"She's a really long story. If she was a book, I'd never finish reading her."

Ms. K laughs. "You have a way with words, Sadie."

"No one has ever said that to me before."

"You're a smart kid. Don't shake your head. I know it's uncomfortable for you to listen to positive things about yourself. But you might have to get a little used to it. You have people who believe you have lots going on inside that somewhat stubborn head of yours. I even have it in writing."

She opens a drawer and takes out Pencilneck's report. If I had known where she was hiding it, I'd have used it to start a nice little bonfire in the backyard.

"You still want me to look at that with you."

"I would have put it the other way around. It's your report to read. If you want me to look at it with you, just let me know." She puts it down on the counter. She's still looking out the window. Everyone looks calm out there. They seem to be having a tea party without any cups. I'm pretty sure I saw Marie feed Hillary a cookie made out of wet sand, which she seems to be eating. Don't know if Ms. K noticed. I should probably say something, but I'm thinking that maybe if they fill up on sand, no one will be eating off my plate tonight but me.

"I might want you to do that. Maybe help me figure out some of Pencilneck's mumbo jumbo."

Since I can't burn it, I might as well try to understand it. It is all about me after all. The story of my life, by Sadie Thompson. And Pencilneck. An action-packed adventure filled with boring information about how super-smart Sadie does and doesn't learn. Should be a bestseller. I just hope there isn't a sequel. No one needs to know any more about me than they already do.

"Just let me know when you're ready. Right now, though, I think maybe you should go out and join the party." The kids are yelling, sounding all excited, and I look out to see who's getting beat up this time. I look at Ms. K, who smiles her smile at me.

"Thanks, Ms. K."

I head outside. Rhiannon is sitting in the sandbox, an excited little kid on each knee. All three of them are chattering at three hundred miles an hour and drinking imaginary tea. I just stand there for a couple of minutes watching and wondering what she's going to say when she sees me.

I take a deep breath and tell myself to stop being such a wuss. Can't believe I'm scared of three little kids covered in sand. I go over to the box and sit down on a tiny triangle seat that digs into my butt and is probably going to give me slivers in unpleasant places. Hillary takes one look at me and plops herself down on my lap, grinning at me like a demented troll with gritty brown teeth and mud drooling down her chin. I'm not sure what to do with her so I just sit really still, hoping she doesn't try to kiss me with her grimy mouth or something gross like that.

Rhiannon looks at me. She doesn't say anything about Tom or about me not coming with her. She doesn't say anything at all. She just hands me a cup made out of air filled with tea made out of her imagination. Cuddling a bit with Marie, she grins at me and raises her own cup into the air.

"Welcome to the party, Sadie."

I don't think I've ever had imaginary tea before. At least not that I remember. Sometimes I wish I could remember more. Maybe if I try talking to Ms. K about my life a little bit sometime it would help me plug up some of the holes in my brain.

But not today. Today I'm going to drink imaginary tea with three grubby fostergirls and decide that it's the first time. Maybe I'll make some new memories. I won't have to worry about remembering them because I can count on Rhiannon to remind me. Over and over and over and over and…

"To fostergirls."

I raise my cup to the sky and take my first drink.

It tastes exactly like sunshine and roses.

Which is not nearly as gross as I expected it to be.

Maybe tomorrow I'll take one of the superbrats' shovels and try a little digging.